D0095315

VALLEY
OF THE EELS

VALLEY OF THE EELS

Written and Illustrated by

Ty Heintze

EAKIN PRESS ★ Austin, Texas

ISBN 0-89015-904-1

Library of Congress Cataloging-in-Publication Data

Heintze, Ty.
  Valley of the Eels : a mystery / written and illustrated by Ty
Heintze.
      p. cm.
  Summary: Young scuba divers Shawn and Billy follow a friendly
dolphin to a domed installation in an ocean canyon, where they
meet a strange creature.
  ISBN 0-89015-904-1 : $14.95
  [1. Dolphins — Fiction. 2. Scuba diving — Fiction. 3. Extraterres-
trial beings — Fiction. 4. Science fiction.] I. Title.
PZ7.H3685Va   1993
[Fic] — dc20   93-2906
                                                                   CIP
                                                                    AC

For my loving wife, Randy.

"Friend," he seemed to say.

Contents

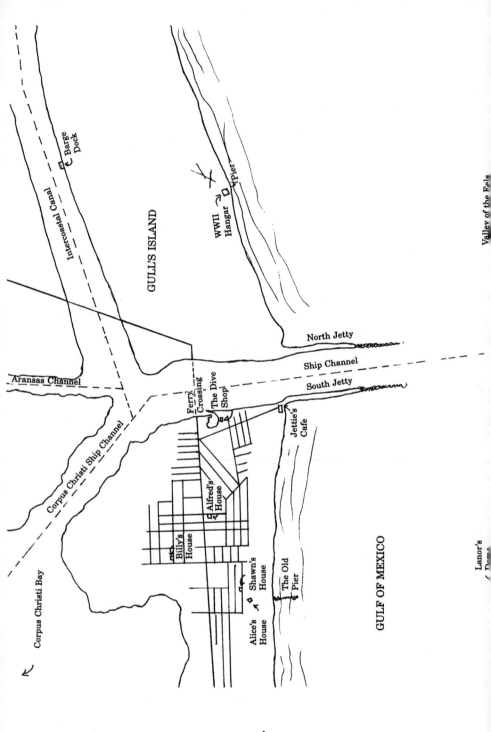

Corpus Christi Bay

Corpus Christi Ship Channel

Aransas Channel

Intercoastal Canal

Barge Dock

GULL'S ISLAND

WWII Hangar

Pier

North Jetty

Ship Channel

South Jetty

Ferry Crossing

The Dive Shop

Jettie's Cafe

Alfred's House

Billy's House

Shawn's House

Alice's House

The Old Pier

GULF OF MEXICO

Valley of the Eels

Lanor's Dome

Author's Note

The setting for *Valley of the Eels* is a small Texas Gulf Coast town very much like Port Aransas, Texas. This small beachtown is located, as is Port Aransas, on a barrier island which separates Corpus Christi Bay from the Gulf of Mexico. Across the ship channel is Gull's Island, much like San Jose Island across from Port Aransas.

A few changes have been made for the purpose of this adventure: The *ferry crossing* has been repositioned so that it crosses onto Gull's Island and then crosses over the intercoastal canal. The *old pier* replaces Horace Caldwell Pier and is moved a mile down the beach. The *Dive Shop* and *Jetties Cafe* are located on property which, in Port Aransas, is controlled by the University of Texas Marine Science Institute. The *World War II hangar* and *pier* have been moved many miles south to the location on Gull's Island.

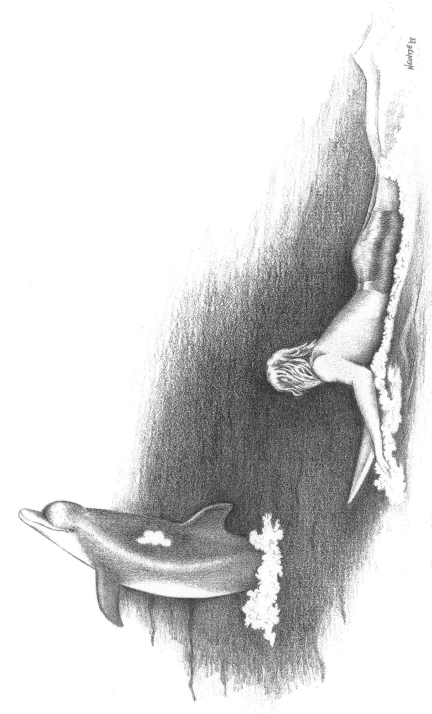

He could sense that Cloud was much more excited than usual.

viii

CHAPTER ONE

"And we won!"

The water felt cool and refreshing as Shawn waded out to the first sandbar. The calm, offshore breeze which nipped at the back of his neck was unseasonable, almost cool. The predawn sky glowed with reds, pinks, and purples as he paddled through the surf.

It was so quiet. Only the sound of the waves and an occasional sea gull broke the silence.

Shawn wheeled around and dropped into his first wave just as a bright orange sun burst above the horizon. And then, right on cue, out of nowhere, Cloud popped through the surface. He was about ten feet ahead of Shawn, moving up and down the face of the wave, making loud whistling noises mixed in with his usual sonar clicks. He'd made these sounds before, when Shawn stroked his back, but this was the first time he'd been so vocal while they surfed.

When Shawn kicked out of the wave, he immediately sensed that Cloud was much more excited than usual. The dolphin came right up to the nose of his surfboard, looked straight into his eyes, and made a distinctly clear sound.

"Friend," he seemed to say. After a brief pause, the dolphin nodded his head and repeated, just as clearly, "Friend."

1

Shawn's mouth fell open. He stared at the dolphin, stunned at what he had heard, or thought he had heard.

Suddenly, Cloud dove, reappearing seconds later as he flew into the air, clicking and whistling. Then, returning to Shawn, he looked him right in the eyes once more and repeated the same unmistakable sound: "Friend."

This time, Shawn managed a reply. "Friend . . . uh . . . you *did* say friend . . . didn't you?"

At this, Cloud shook his head up and down, sonared a barrage of clicks, and once again sounded: *"Friend."*

"Okay . . . Friend!" Shawn replied immediately, and reached out to stroke Cloud's head. He ran his hand along the dolphin's back, over the cloud-like marking near his dorsal fin, and up to his slippery forehead.

Just then, Billy's voice broke through the sound of the breaking waves. "Shawn . . . Shawn!" he yelled. "Come in! I have *unreal news!* Come in!" Back on the beach, Billy was jumping wildly, waving his arms and screaming from the top of his lungs. "Come in, Shawn . . . Come in!"

"Okay," Shawn yelled. "Keep your shirt on." He turned just in time to see the dolphin dive and swim away. Cloud always left when anyone else came near. Shawn hadn't even told Billy about the dolphin, for fear Cloud might be scared away. Now he was feeling even more protective of their relationship. His head was still spinning as he turned to catch the next wave in.

Did I really hear Cloud say "friend"? he thought. *Naw, it was probably just a noise that sounded like friend.*

* * *

Billy had a smile on his face that stretched from ear to ear. He looked like he'd just won a million dollars or found a buried treasure chest.

"Remember last month when we bought the raffle tickets at Johnson's Dive Shop for a bunch of diving gear?" he yelled as Shawn coasted in on the shorebreak.

2

Shawn vaguely remembered filling out the tickets. "Oh, yeah. We bought tickets two different times — so we'd have a double chance of winning."

"Right!" Billy screeched. "And *we* won! You and I, and some girl named Alice. Do you believe it? New diving gear!"

"We won?" Shawn screamed. *"Both* of us?" He grabbed Billy's shoulders and they jumped up and down, hollering, until both fell, exhausted, on the wet sand.

"Wait a minute!" Shawn broke in, half out of breath. "We'd better go over to the Dive Shop and make sure it's true."

"Right!" Billy agreed, panting. "I saw our names on the bulletin board at the Jetties Cafe, but you're right. Let's go!"

"Meet me at my house in fifteen minutes," Shawn said, grabbing his board.

"Okay," Billy answered. "I'm taking my board home too. *Who-o-o-a-a-ow!*" he yelled. "New diving gear. *Unreal!* Fifteen minutes — at your house. *Wh-o-o-a-a-ow!*"

* * *

Shawn couldn't seem to walk fast enough. He was so excited about winning the raffle, he'd almost forgotten about Cloud.

Incredible, he thought. *How could the dolphin know how to sound out a word — in English? Maybe he escaped from Sea World, or one of those aquariums that train dolphins. Yeah — that* must *be it. How else could a dolphin know a word?* Cutting across the dunes to Second Street, his thoughts rambled on. *I always thought Cloud was special, the way he showed up every morning and let me pet him. But a talking dolphin? Who'd believe me? Even if I did* tell *anyone.*

He laid his surfboard next to the big freezer on the back porch, grabbed the water jug out of the old icebox, and burst through the kitchen door.

3

"Shawn, is that you?" his mother called from upstairs.

"Yes, ma'am!" he answered, almost yelling. "You won't believe what happened! Billy and I won the raffle at the Dive Shop! We both won new *scuba* gear!" He was talking so fast, his words ran together.

"You *what*?" she asked, making her way down the creaky wooden staircase.

Shawn repeated the good news as he passed her on the stairs.

"Well, that sounds like a dream come true, son. When do you get this new gear?"

"We're going down to the Dive Shop now to find out!" he answered, hurriedly. "Do you think you could make us a couple of sandwiches real quick? Please, Mom?"

"Oh, all right. I'll make you some sandwiches if you'll just slow down a little."

She was opening a bag of chips when Billy came flying through the kitchen door.

"Oh, hello, Mrs. Anderson. Where's Shawn? Did he tell you?"

"Yes, Billy, he told me. It sounds almost too good to be true." She laid napkins by their plates and went to the cabinet for glasses. "Have a seat, young man," she said. "Would you like tea or water?"

"Tea'll be fine, ma'am. Thank you."

About that time Shawn slid down the banister and into the kitchen, drawing a disapproving glare from Mrs. Anderson. "Thanks, Mom," he said.

"I said to slow down," she cautioned. "Now, eat your food properly, and don't —" The buzzer on the washing machine stopped her in midsentence. She turned and left the room, mumbling. "What's the use? I might as well be talking to myself."

The boys grinned at each other, wolfed down the sandwiches, and were out the back door in a flash.

"Slow down, you two!" they could hear her calling after them. "Watch out for traffic!"

4

CHAPTER TWO

The Dive Shop

In no time at all they were locking their bikes in front of the Dive Shop.

"Shawn, look at the poster on the front door."

"You know, I still feel like I'm dreaming all of this," Shawn replied. "I mean, out of all those tickets Mr. John-

5

son sold over the past two months, how could you and I have won first and second prize?"

Billy was quick with an answer. "I don't know, but I'm sure not going to question it." That ear-to-ear smile returned. Shawn was sporting one of his own as they pulled open the heavy glass door.

"*Oh no!*" Shawn cringed, glancing at Billy, sharing an instant of pure disgust. "*Alfred Karbunkle!*" they moaned, a beam of telepathic energy fusing their eyes. They wondered if they were ever going to shake this guy. It wasn't bad enough that they had to sit next to Alfred in almost every class last year, listening to his constant "know-it-all" chatter and endless practical jokes that seldom worked. And they had endured his persistent attempts to horn into whatever they were up to after school, always making a complete nuisance of himself. No, that wasn't bad enough. Now he was even following them around the beach, ruining their summer vacation.

Summer is when you're supposed to get a break from teachers and *Alfred,* Shawn thought to himself.

"*You make me sick!*" Alfred growled, scowling through squinty eyes.

Shawn jerked his head back a notch. *That's a switch,* he thought. We *make* him *sick?*

Billy nudged Shawn's arm with his elbow. "Do you *believe* this?" he snickered.

Alfred grumbled through his teeth. "My dad talked *all* our relatives into buying raffle tickets for me! I've got *fourteen* tickets!" he glared, holding up the crumpled wad of losing stubs.

Mr. Johnson's raspy voice broke in just as Billy opened his mouth to reply. "Shawn . . . Billy . . . glad you came by. Why weren't you at the drawin' last night?"

The boys spun around to see the old man's sun-bleached mustache curl up as he smiled.

"Hey, Mr. J.," Billy answered. "We really didn't think we had any chance of winning. To tell the truth, we'd completely forgotten about the raffle."

Alfred sneered, "I'll *bet* you forgot."

"Really!" Billy continued, pretending Alfred wasn't even there. "If I hadn't seen our names posted over at the cafe, we still wouldn't know!"

"Well," the bronze-skinned old sailor grinned, "I guess you'll want to see what you won?"

"Yes, sir!" Shawn burst out. "Billy and I have wanted our own gear for the longest time. Uh — not that your rental gear isn't the best, Mr. J."

Alfred leaned in, wincing his face into a mocking grin. "We've always wanted our own gear, Mr. J.," he jeered.

Billy turned his back to Alfred. "Say, Mr. J.," he said, winking at Shawn, "are you planning any trips out to the oil rigs soon?"

"Next week," Mr. Johnson replied, raising his eyebrows a twitch. "Why? Do you fellas want to sign up for it? Most everyone's goin', but there's still room."

"How much does it cost?" Billy asked, looking into the old man's weathered eyes.

"Well, I'll tell you what," he paused, twisting his long mustache between his fingers. "If you fellas want to help me with the light-bar for the camera ..." He paused again. "I'll throw in the trip to the rigs with your prizes."

"Sure, we'll help! Won't we, Shawn?"

"Of course! What day next week?"

"Tuesday mornin' bright an' early. We'll be back around noon."

Billy held up his new regulator and mask. "Is this really *all ours*, Mr. J.? *Unreal!*"

Alfred's presence had almost been forgotten when his pestering, whining voice popped in again. "Is this really all ours?" he mimicked.

Shawn turned into his own thoughts. *Mom's right. This* is *like a dream come true. Now I can go diving with Cloud. But I wonder if he'll still know me without the surfboard — and with scuba gear and bubbles?*

7

Mr. Johnson's hand on Shawn's shoulder brought him out of the daydream. "You fellas have been divin' with us for two summers now." His hand tightened as he spoke. "So I think you can handle this gear without any problems. Just remember, always go divin' with a buddy — and always tell someone where you're goin' and how long you plan to be down."

"Don't worry, Mr. J.," Shawn answered. "We'll either sign out with you or our parents. They always want to know everything we do anyway."

"Can we use your phone?" Billy interrupted. "We need to call our dads so they can pick up our gear after work."

"You bet," Mr. Johnson nodded. "Go on back to the tank room and sign up for the trip with Bob. You can use the phone on the work bench."

* * *

Shawn was leaning on the porch railing of his house, nervously tapping his fingers, when his dad pulled into the driveway. Bounding off the porch and into the back of the truck in a blur, he found even more than he was expecting. Both sets of scuba gear were stuffed into a big cardboard box next to two air tanks.

Mr. Anderson spoke first. "I went ahead and picked up two tanks," he said. "I'll take you out in the morning to test this stuff out. I'm taking the day off."

"Can Billy go too?" Shawn blurted out.

"Of course. That's why I got two tanks and brought Billy's gear along. We'll go out past the old pier."

"Are you going diving with us?" Shawn hoped.

"Get serious, son. You know the doc put a halt to that after my stroke. No, I'm after some trout." He started walking to the house, talking over his shoulder. "I've already spoken with Billy's dad, but you'd better call Billy anyway. Tell him to be here early. We'll leave around six A.M."

8

CHAPTER THREE

"Amazing!"

As they were driving to the docks the next morning, Shawn couldn't stop thinking about Cloud and how ironic it was that Dad wanted to go fishing near the same spot where he surfed with the dolphin. He wondered if Cloud would be there, and whether the dolphin would recognize him or stay when he saw Billy.

"You guys stow the gear in the cabin," Shawn's dad said, forcing the key into the rusty padlock. "I'll fill up the ice chest and get some drinks. Shawn, check the gas tank. I think it's full, but make sure before we leave."

"Okay, Dad."

"Billy," he continued. "How about running over to the bait stand for some live shrimp? Here's the money. The bait-box is with the fishing gear."

"Sure thing, Mr. Anderson."

*   *   *

The sun was already well above the horizon when Shawn's father dropped anchor about fifty yards from the old pier. It was another calm morning with a slight southerly breeze.

"You guys *do* want to fish for a while before you go diving, don't you?" Dad asked, grinning. He knew they

9

could hardly wait to get that new gear on.

"Are you kidding?" Shawn answered, shaking his head.

Mr. Anderson laughed, pulled off his T-shirt, and reached in the ice chest for a cold soda. "Okay," he chuckled. "Just thought I'd ask."

Billy was already handing the air tanks up to Shawn. They helped each other sort things out, adjust straps, and check the pressure gauges while Mr. Anderson readied his rod and reel, attaching a new leader.

"Such a beautiful morning for fishing," Mr. Anderson said. "The water's pretty clear too. You guys should have a good day below." Looking back at the two boys eagerly working together, he felt a tinge of pride. They were taking things so seriously, checking each other's regulators and all the connections on the hoses. When they were almost ready to go into the water, he grinned, reached into his pocket, and pulled out a new diving watch. "I thought you might need this."

Shawn's eyes lit up. "Incredible! Thanks, Dad! We were looking at one just like this at the Dive Shop, yesterday."

"Oh, by the way—that represents your allowance for the rest of the summer. Take good care of it."

Man, Shawn thought. *I must have done something right—somewhere.* He looked up. "What next?"

"Set it for twenty minutes, Shawn," his dad continued. "I want you to keep the boat in sight at least that long. Then, come up and let me know how the gear is checking out."

"Okay, Dad. Twenty minutes—done."

"You don't have to worry about us, Mr. Anderson," Billy interrupted. "This is all new stuff. We've never had it so good."

"Twenty minutes," Shawn's dad repeated, sternly.

"Right," Billy quickly conceded. "Ready, Shawn?"

They backed up to the side of the boat, adjusted their masks, and fell into the cool, quiet water of the Gulf of

Mexico. Dad was right. The water *was* unusually clear today. Shawn could see all the way to the bottom of the anchor line, four fathoms down. Big, ugly-looking crabs were crawling on the bottom, and seven or eight dark gray stingrays hovered nearby. Shawn thought they looked like birds flapping their wings, flying through the water.

Turning, he saw Billy skimming the bottom, grabbing at the sand from time to time. *He always thinks he's going to find a Spanish coin, or an old shipwreck,* Shawn thought. Billy *had* found a couple of square nails one time. When they took them to the Science Museum in Corpus Christi, the curator said the nails might be from a sixteenth-century Spanish galleon. Ever since that day, Billy talked about finding gold coins — and maybe even a whole shipwreck. Mr. Johnson had nicknamed him "Treasure Map" because Billy was always trying to get him to make the club dives in areas where he thought a sunken ship might be sitting, just waiting to be discovered.

Looking up toward the boat, Shawn saw a school of mullet popping their heads through the surface, curious about what was going on in *their* ocean. Then, suddenly, he sensed something approaching from his left. It was a gray and white blur. Before he knew what had happened, it was swimming off. He could see now that it was a dolphin, but he couldn't tell if it was Cloud or not. Just then, another dolphin swam by — and then another, and another. Four in all went by, but didn't show any interest in the boys. Shawn thought they might be headed for the pier.

At that instant, he felt something pulling on his arm. It was Billy, motioning for Shawn to follow. They swam over to a thick piece of what seemed to be wood protruding from the sandy bottom. The wood was dark brown, almost black, with round holes, spaced evenly. Billy started digging at the sand, trying to free it, and Shawn joined in — but it was soon evident that the ocean floor wasn't ready to give it up yet.

Glancing at his new watch, Shawn noticed that fifteen minutes had gone by, even though it had seemed like only five. He tapped Billy on the shoulder and pointed up to the boat.

Mr. Anderson was leaning back in his deck chair, enjoying the warm sunshine, when the boys broke through the surface. He looked at his watch and smiled. "How's it goin'?" he asked.

"Great, Dad. Everything's working perfectly. Right, Billy?"

"Right. Say, Mr. Anderson, you wouldn't have a little shovel or something I could dig with, would you?"

"A shovel? What in the world do you want a shovel for?"

"There's a piece of old wood sticking out of the sand down here. I think it's part of an old ship or something."

"Yeah, Dad. He really did find something that looks old. It's a real thick board with round holes — about this big." He made a circle with his thumb and finger.

"I know — maybe a big spoon from the galley!" Billy interrupted.

"Hang on, I'll look." He came back with a soup ladle and a butter knife. "This'll have to do. We don't do much planting on the boat."

"Sure, this is better than bare fingers. Right, Shawn?"

Ten minutes later, they had stirred up so much of the fine-grain sand, Shawn couldn't even see where he was digging. Backpedaling out of the murky cloud, he bumped into something that pushed back. Nervously, he veered to one side, pushing his legs as hard and fast as they would go — back farther and farther — until he could see three large, dark forms inside the sand-cloud with Billy. *Sharks?* he thought. *Billy, get out of there!*

At that instant, from Shawn's left, came such a loud burst of *clicks* and *bangs* that he had to cover his ears.

Click . . . click . . . click . . . BANG! Click . . . click . . . click . . . BANG! Click . . . BANG! BANG! Click-click . . .

12

click . . . BANG! It sounded like firecrackers mixed in with sonar clicks.

Unreal, Shawn thought, pressing his fingers into his ears so hard that it hurt, trying to muffle the sound of the intermittent *bangs. It's dolphins! What are they doing? How are they making those sounds—like explosions?*

Billy emerged from the cloud in a flurry, his hands pressed to his ears, as three large bull sharks hurried away from the approaching dolphins.

Cloud—it's you! Shawn thought, as they passed, still clicking and banging. The dolphins pursued the sharks until they were well out of sight and then returned, whistling softly.

Cloud swam near Shawn, sonared a short blast of clicks, and then stopped, hanging motionless in the water.

It's me, fella, Shawn said in his mind.

The dolphin eased closer, staring into Shawn's face mask, clicking softly.

Shawn reached out cautiously and touched Cloud's forehead, stroking it gently. *See, Cloud . . . It's your old friend, Shawn.*

Cloud nuzzled his head into Shawn's hand, his dolphin eyes smiling with an uncanny human quality.

Then, as quickly as they'd come to the boys' rescue, the other three dolphins turned and swam away. Cloud didn't seem to notice, or didn't care, as long as Shawn rubbed behind his eyes and along his back.

By now, Billy had summoned up enough courage to join Shawn. He reached out, looking first at Shawn for a last minute nod of reassurance, and touched the dolphin's side.

Cloud looked at Billy, then turned back to Shawn and hummed softly.

That's right, Cloud. This is Billy . . . my friend.

Sonaring faintly, the dolphin then whistled a few low tones and carefully maneuvered clear of the boys.

What's the matter, fella? Had enough? Shawn thought.

13

Cloud seemed to answer with a short melody of whistles and clicks, then swam about ten feet away and started nodding his head from side to side, whistling all the while.

What's up? What are you trying to say, Cloud? Shawn wondered.

Then the dolphin swam back to Shawn, looped around behind him, and gave his back a slight nudge. Immediately following this gentle bit of encouragement, Cloud once again swam ten feet out and resumed his whistling melody.

Do you want us to follow you? Is that *what you're trying to tell us?*

Cloud's nodding instantly changed to an up and down motion, as if he'd read Shawn's thoughts and was answering.

Unreal! This dolphin is too much. Shawn looked at Billy and pointed at the dolphin. Then he motioned for Billy to follow him.

As they drew near the beckoning dolphin, Cloud turned and swam another fifteen feet, stopped, and urged them on with his melody.

They followed, again and again, as he led them farther and farther away from the boat.

Where are we going, Cloud? thought Shawn. *We can't follow you forever, you know. We only have so much air . . . Uh-oh.* He jerked back, grabbing his pressure gauge. *Yeah — we'd better turn around.* He held his hand out in front of Billy's face, pointing to his watch. Billy shrugged his shoulders.

Shawn nodded that it was time to go.

Cloud's whistling intensified when they slowed and turned back in the direction of the boat. He hurried over, looped them a few times, and then swam out again, clicking and whistling stubbornly.

Sorry, fella. We've got to get back. Shawn glanced at his pressure gauge. They had only ten minutes worth of air left.

"There were three other dolphins at first," Shawn added.

Cloud persisted, but to no avail, as the boys made a beeline to the boat. Finally, the dolphin gave in and caught up with them.

Yeah, Shawn gestured. *Come with us, Cloud.*

*   *   *

Most of the sand had settled by the time they passed over their "find," and they started a slow ascent. The water felt warmer, inch by inch, as they drew near the starboard side of the boat, surprising a wandering school of trout.

Mr. Anderson was a bit startled when the boys unexpectedly broke through the surface. But he was even more startled when the dolphin popped up between them.

"Dad! Look at this dolphin!" Shawn yelled, ripping off his mouthpiece and mask. Yes, he *was* spilling the beans about the dolphin. But it seemed like Cloud was ready to meet new people, and Shawn felt good about it.

"*Well,* this is interesting," Mr. Anderson mumbled to himself, leaning over the side. "He sure is friendly," he said. "How long has he been with you?"

"Since he scared the sharks away!" Billy blurted out.

"There were three other dolphins at first," Shawn added. "But they left — and this one stayed."

"Wait a minute, now — back up. What's this about sharks — and three more dolphins?"

The boys described how the dolphins had frightened the bull sharks away with their loud clicking and banging. And they explained how *this* dolphin had tried to lead them out into the Gulf.

"That loud banging noise," Mr. Anderson said, helping the boys back into the boat, "is what they do to stun their prey."

"You mean they can stun the sharks, Dad?"

"No, not the ones you described. They probably only annoyed those guys. No, it was the dolphin's aggressive

16

behavior—along with the loud banging—that made the sharks leave." Mr. Anderson glanced back at the dolphin, grinned, and gave him a wink the boys couldn't see. Cloud whistled sharply, came halfway out of the water, and backpedaled on his tail, nodding his head up and down.

"Hey—look, Shawn!" Billy yelled. "He's trying to get us to follow him again!"

"Amazing," Shawn's father sighed.

CHAPTER FOUR

"I think we should follow him!"

Early the next morning Shawn and Billy were loading the diving gear into Mr. Anderson's truck.

"Hey, Shawn. Do you still have that army surplus shovel? You know — the little one that folds up."

"You mean the trench shovel? Yeah, it's right over here — in the garage."

"Let's take it to dig with."

"*You* can take it if you want to," Shawn grumbled. "I'm not lugging this thing along. Besides, the sand'll just get stirred up again and then settle back."

"Yeah, I was thinking about that too. And I think I have an idea. At least, I'm going to give it a try."

"Uh-oh, another Shelton brainstorm, huh? Watch out."

"No, really. This is a good idea. Look," he insisted, opening his red nylon specimen bag. "I brought a bunch of my mom's two-gallon freezer bags. I'll scoop the sand into the bags, seal them up, and then we can take them a few feet away and dump them out. What do you think?"

"Sounds like a lot of work to me."

"But it'll be worth it," Billy persisted. "Just think — we might be digging up the remains of an old Spanish galleon, or maybe it was just a trade ship. Anyway, there might be some gold coins — or silver."

"Okay — we'll try it. But first we've got to talk Dad

into taking us by the Dive Shop for some full tanks."

"Think he'll do it?"

"We'll see. Here he comes now."

Mr. Anderson grinned when he saw the boys perched on the tailgate of his truck. "Well, what do we have here?"

"Good morning, Dad!"

"Hi, Mr. Anderson. Beautiful mornin', isn't it?"

"Yes, it *is* a beautiful morning. What are you guys up to?"

"Well, Dad . . . could you *ple-a-s-e* take just a couple of minutes to run us by the Dive Shop? We need air. And it's free—it came with our prizes. Come on, Dad. Please?"

"All right, all right," Mr. Anderson answered, a curious grin trying to show itself in his eyes. "But you boys had better be quick as a flash. I can't be foolin' with you two all morning. Get into the cab with me. I don't want you riding in the back."

"You got it! Thanks, Dad. I owe you one!"

"You owe me more than one," he chuckled.

"Oh, you know what I mean, Dad. I'd do anything for you." He snuck a wink at Billy. "You know that."

"Well, you're going to have a chance to prove that pretty soon," Dad grinned, raising his eyebrows.

"What do you mean?" Shawn grimaced.

"Oh, just a few chores around the house. But I want *you* to start taking the responsibility of remembering to do them—without me or your mother reminding you."

Gopher guts, Shawn thought. *Oh well, I guess I knew something like this was coming.*

"Now," his dad said, as he pulled up to the side door of the shop, "get in there and get out—quick."

They were in and back in just minutes, panting like poodles, as they jumped into the truck and slammed the door shut.

"Okay, Dad, we're ready if you are."

"Where to?"

"By the old pier. We're going to try to dig up that wood we found yesterday."

19

"Is that right? Well, try to find that soup ladle you dropped, Billy."

"I'll find it, Mr. Anderson, don't worry."

"So, you guys think you've found something special, huh?"

"Yes, sir," Billy answered. "I looked in my books about ships last night—old Spanish ships and stuff. Anyway, this wood looks like maybe it was a rail from the main deck of an old square-rigger. It has round holes in it, like the ones they put belaying pins into. You know what they are, don't you? They're big, round wooden pegs they secured lines with."

Billy would have rambled on forever, but fortunately Mr. Anderson was already pulling up to the old pier.

"Think they'll ever rebuild this thing?" Shawn interrupted, winking at his dad.

"Probably not, son . . . unless they use cement." He turned off the engine. "Hurricanes knock them down too easily."

Billy was still mumbling about the shipwreck as he popped the door open, swinging out on it like a monkey on a vine.

"Don't do that, Billy!" Dad scowled. "You'll mess up the hinges!"

"Sorry, Mr. Anderson. I forgot."

* * *

Locating the piece of wood turned out to be more difficult than they had expected. Half an hour's worth of air was already gone, and they hadn't come across anything resembling Billy's ship rail.

Suddenly, Billy veered to his right and started poking in the sand.

All right . . . finally! Shawn thought as he hurried over.

Billy was already breaking out the plastic bags. He handed one to Shawn and started filling it with sand immediately. Three or four scoops was all it would hold. Shawn sealed the bag and held another open for Billy to fill. This went on until ten bags were filled, sealed, and sitting on the bottom.

Shawn gestured that that was enough for now. He cradled one bag in his left arm and grabbed another.

It wasn't easy, swimming with two full bags, but they managed to carry them a good twenty feet before dumping the sand.

This could take forever, Shawn thought. *But the biggest problem is finding the dumb thing.* He looked at his pressure gauge. *Yeah, just as I thought . . . we've already used most of our air. Only ten minutes left.*

Just then, Cloud made his entrance, whistling and clicking cheerfully. He swam by Shawn, nodding his head, and nudged Billy on his shoulder as he passed. Then he stopped about ten feet out.

Here we go again, Shawn thought, motioning for the dolphin to come to him.

At this, Cloud began his beckoning melody, nodding his head from side to side, just as he'd done before.

Shawn knew that Cloud wanted them to follow him again. Cloud whistled a little louder, swam out another five or six feet, and repeated his melody.

Sorry, fella, we're out of air. You came too late, Shawn thought. *Besides, I've got to figure out a way to mark this thing so we won't have to waste much air looking for it. Wait . . . that's it! Air!* He reached into his blue specimen bag and pulled out a short length of nylon cord. *I can make a buoy with one of the empty bags and this line.*

Amidst Cloud's noisy beckoning, Shawn tapped on Billy's shoulder and pointed to his watch. Billy looked as if he didn't want to believe it, but reluctantly he laid the shovel down and took the last two full bags to be dumped. When he returned, Shawn motioned for him to be still for a minute while he held one of the empty bags over Billy's escaping air bubbles. In just seconds the inverted bag was filled with trapped air. Shawn squeezed the open end

21

shut and tied the line to it. *There,* he thought, *an under-water balloon buoy.* Slipping the other end through one of the belaying pin holes, he secured the makeshift buoy and backed up to admire his handiwork.

Billy gave a double thumbs-up and nodded as he turned the other empty bags inside out, dumping out the last grains of fine sand.

By this time, Cloud was visibly upset with the two treasure hunters. His melody intensified to an incessant chattering and scolding.

Cloud . . . cool it! We can't go with you. Shawn pointed toward the shore and Billy followed, grabbing the shovel and thumping the buoy as he passed it.

Come on, Cloud . . . swim with us. We'll be back tomorrow. Maybe we'll go with you then, Shawn thought as he looked back over his shoulder. The dolphin was following, clicking softly. He almost sounded depressed — that is, if dolphins get depressed. *Cheer up, Cloud . . . We'll be back . . . You'll see.*

* * *

It was past 11:00 and the boys were still sitting on the beach waiting for Billy's mom to pick them up.

"I think we should follow him tomorrow," Shawn said, tossing a bit of broken shell into the shorebreak.

"Yeah . . . I guess we could do that. But I want to do some more digging too. We were just starting to make progress."

"Yuk," Shawn said as he readied another shell fragment. "What's this?"

A brown, frothy foam was washing in with the tide. And with it were dead fish, bloated and belly up.

"*Pee-uuu!* Catch a whiff of that!" Billy grumbled. "Disgusting!"

They both jumped to their feet, covering their noses as if it would help.

"Look, Shelton, hundreds of them!" shouted Shawn.

22

"Wonder what the brown stuff is? Red tide or something?"

"I don't know, but here comes your mom. Let's get out of here."

* * *

Mrs. Shelton told the boys that she had just heard a special news report on the radio about an unusual fish kill. "They were saying that thousands of dead fish and eels were washing ashore down by the jetties. The people from the University Marine Science Lab don't have the answer yet . . . said they're going to have to do some tests on the fish."

"Did they say anything about red tide, Mom?"

"They just said it wasn't the same stuff we had a few years ago."

"Weird," Shawn sighed as they pulled into his driveway.

Half an hour later, they were stowing the gear in Shawn's garage when Alfred rode up on his black dune bike, skidding on the loose shell.

"Hey, Shawn . . . Billy! Did you hear about the fish kill?"

Oh, wonderful, Shawn thought. *Not you again.*

"Yeah, we saw it," Billy retorted. "Just a bunch of stinky fish."

"So y'all have already been to the beach, huh? Did you go diving already?" He didn't sound as whiny as yesterday, but that nosey, prying voice couldn't be camouflaged.

"Get a life," Billy scoffed. "Isn't your mother calling you or something?"

"What is it with y'all? Why don't you like me? I've never done anything to you!" Alfred persisted.

"Oh, I don't know, Alfred," Shawn spoke up, trying not to sound as cutting as Billy had. "I guess it's because you're always bugging us."

23

"I just want to be your friend."

"Yeah . . . well —" Billy started, but Shawn cut him off.

"Tell you what, Alfred. You leave us alone for a few days and we'll come find you sometime — and go riding back in the dunes or something."

"Really?" Alfred perked up. "I know a really neat secret place over on Gull's Island. It's a —"

"That's all government property," Billy interrupted, "you can't go over there."

"I go there all the time," Alfred boasted. "There's a neat old World War Two —" He didn't finish his sentence, stopping abruptly. "Well, it's a secret. But I'll show you if you want to go now."

"Now?" Billy nagged. "Why now?"

"Cool it, Shelton. You're beginning to sound like you-know-who," Shawn whispered and then turned back to Alfred. "Okay, Alfred. Show us your secret."

Billy glared at Shawn.

"Come on, Billy," Shawn winked, "let's go see Alfred's secret place."

"Oh, all right," Billy grumbled. "But how can we get through those big gates? They're always locked, or there's a guard."

"Just follow me," Alfred smiled. "I know a way. First we have to ride the ferry across the channel." He couldn't believe it. Finally, he had some friends to share his secret.

* * *

Noisy gulls hovered overhead, begging morsels from tourists, as the ferry slowly inched its way across the ship channel. The sky had turned a dark gray, and thunderstorms rumbled in the distance.

"Looks like we might get a little wet," Billy complained.

"Lighten up, Shelton. You won't melt." Shawn had decided that this little trek to Gull's Island wasn't going

24

to be so bad, even if Alfred *was* leading the way. After all, neither he nor Billy had ever been brave enough to go there before. They had heard that the navy practiced shelling the island from ships out in the Gulf, and that live rounds could be buried in the sand. Maybe that was Alfred's secret, the boys guessed. Maybe he had found a bunch of unexploded projectiles or something.

"Don't worry, Billy," Alfred grinned. "Where we're going, we can get in out of the rain."

"What are you talking about?" Billy quizzed, not quite as sarcastically as before.

"Yeah, Alfred," Shawn winked, poking him lightly on the shoulder. "What's the big secret?"

"Just wait," Alfred teased. "We'll be there before it starts raining." For once he had the boys curious about something only *he* knew, and he was loving every minute of it.

The ferry soon docked on the other side of the channel, and the three boys were the first ones off. Alfred turned sharply to the right when he cleared the loading ramp, riding along the cement embankment. It was only three feet wide, so they had to pay close attention to what they were doing. Even Billy remained silent. Then, just as they were approaching the tall, chain-link fence that protruded out over the embankment, Alfred swerved to the left, following a path through a washout behind the cement wall. It was just deep enough for the boys to ride under the fence and into a slight valley between the dunes.

Shawn was smiling when he looked back over his shoulder at Billy. "All *right!* Huh, Shelton?" he yelled.

Billy was grinning too. "Yeah!" he called back. "Secret mission coming up!" He was liking this excursion as much as Shawn was, even if he had a hard time admitting it.

A barrage of screeching gulls drowned out everything as the three sped through a large flock that had been quietly resting in the dunes. The noise was deafening as the surprised gulls scurried about, making it known in no uncertain terms that the boys were not welcome on their island.

The path through the dunes opened up onto a flat stretch of hard-packed sand, littered with driftwood, old tires, and rusty pieces of metal sticking up at angles from the sand.

Alfred didn't slow his pace or look back. He knew they were following, and he seemed as anxious to get to his secret spot as they were. A few hundred feet farther and they were in the dunes again, following another path which Alfred obviously knew quite well. Suddenly it opened up again, revealing an old, abandoned World War Two landing strip and airplane hangar. Another smaller building, probably what had been the barracks, had almost collapsed and was covered with sea gull droppings. Signs posted all around the hangar were old and rusted and could barely be read: "GOVERNMENT PROPERTY . . . NO TRESPASSING." A dilapidated old walkway led to a pier about fifty yards behind the hangar. The pier looked as old as everything else, but it wasn't falling apart like the walkway and the barracks. The hangar was boarded up with chains and locks on the huge doors that stretched from the ground to the very top of the building.

"Well, what do you think?" Alfred beamed.

W-h-a-c-k! P-o-w! W-h-a-c-k! Rumble . . . rumble . . . rumble . . . rumble . . . A bolt of lightning struck so near that all three boys jerked back, hearts pounding. Adrenaline pumped through their skinny bodies so fast that it took the words right out of their mouths. Heavy, cold raindrops smashed against their faces, soaking them to the bones in seconds.

Alfred moved first. He scrambled to the far end of the hangar and slipped through a broken hinge. Shawn and Billy were close on his heels.

W-h-a-c-k! P-o-w! P-o-w! Rumble-rumble . . . Another bolt slammed onto the island, reverberating and echoing

26

inside the hangar.

The boys stood motionless, staring at each other with wide eyes, until Shawn nervously peeled off his wet T-shirt, kicked off his drenched tennis shoes, and took a deep breath. "Sounds like somebody up there is telling us we're not supposed to be here," he mumbled.

Billy's teeth began to chatter. "This is *intense!*" His shirt sleeve tore as the saturated cloth clung to his skin. "Oh, great!" he grumbled, flinging it over his bike.

A nervous laughter broke the tension as Alfred turned and walked into the cavernous building, waving for Shawn and Billy to follow.

*   *   *

An hour later, the rain was still pounding against the roof of the dusty, ramshackle old hangar. The boys hadn't noticed how much time had passed because there was so much to explore. Two P-51 Mustangs sat partially disassembled amidst an array of airplane parts, wooden step ladders, and vintage power tools from a time long past. Huge cabinets were still full of nuts and bolts, gauges of all sorts, and small hand tools with wooden handles.

The boys' clothes were mostly dry by now, but no one had stopped long enough to check on them. Billy had a pile of odds and ends he had claimed. Shawn was folding some old coastal charts into a bundle and Alfred was trying to dismantle a compass from the instrument panel of one of the planes when they heard a new sound.

RrrrRrrrRrrrRrrrRrrrrrrrrRrrrRrrrRrrrrrrrr!

The lightning and thunder had stopped long ago, and the rain was diminishing, but a new muffled rumbling was gradually increasing in volume.

"It's a boat," Billy whispered. Even his whisper carried across the hollow building to Shawn. Alfred popped his head out of the cockpit.

The noise was getting closer and closer, louder and louder, until it sounded as if it was right next to the han-

27

gar. The boys scurried about like frightened mice, searching for a vantage point, but all the windows were either boarded-up or covered with such a thick coating of salt and grime that they couldn't see through. Alfred, however, found one small pane of glass so loose in its caulking that it easily fell into his hands.

"Shawn . . . Billy," he whispered. "Over here."

They peered out the opening, through the drizzling rain, to see an oil-rig supply boat pulling up to the pier. Two scruffy-looking sailors jumped onto the platform and secured the bow and stern lines. A tall, dark-skinned man stepped out of the wheelhouse, running his fingers through his long, black beard—the only hair on his head. He didn't even have eyebrows. Quickly, this ominous figure of a man pulled a black baseball cap out of his hip pocket to cover his bald head from the rain. Then he just stood there, watching the sailors.

The men didn't talk. They set about their task like it was routine. Several large, wooden crates were stacked on the pier, which they promptly loaded onto the fantail of the boat. As soon as this was done, they loosened the lines securing the boat and jumped back aboard. The instant their feet hit the deck, the craft sped away.

"I wonder what that's all about?" Alfred mumbled. "I've never seen *them* here before."

"Something doesn't seem right," Shawn sighed, looking at Billy. "Do you know what I mean?"

"Yeah," Billy agreed. "I get the same feeling. Like they were in a hurry to get away — as quick as they could."

"I didn't see any military markings on the boat," Shawn added, rubbing his arms.

"And they weren't wearing uniforms," Alfred broke in.

"Weird, huh?" Shawn sighed. An eerie feeling hung in the air. Did they just see something they weren't supposed to see?

At just that instant, the rain stopped and the sun

came out.

Billy walked over to the bicycles. "Hey, Shawn. Our clothes are dry. Let's go. What do you say?"

"Yeah, let's go," Alfred piped up. He wanted it to be his idea to leave. After all, this was *his* secret place. "But guys," he continued, "before we go, uh, you *are* going to keep this place a secret, aren't you? I mean, if anyone finds out that we've been here, we might get into a lot of trouble."

"Sure," Shawn assured him. "Tell you what. We'll call this place G.I.S. whenever we talk about it." He turned to Billy. "Okay, Shelton?"

"Sure, but what does G.I.S. mean?"

"Gull's Island Secret, what else?" Shawn grinned and turned back to Alfred. "How about it, Alfred?"

Alfred smiled. "Okay . . . yeah, that sounds great . . . G.I.S. No one will ever suspect what that means. And we never come here alone — always the three of us. Deal?"

"Deal," Shawn nodded.

"Deal, Alfred," Billy agreed. "Now, let's hit the road."

* * *

By the time they had crammed all the loot they could carry into their pockets and socks, and slithered through the broken hangar door, the sun was shining brightly and the rain had already soaked into the sand, packing it even tighter.

The trip back across the channel was a quiet one. Each boy was turning inward a little, thinking over what had happened that afternoon. When they split up after stopping for a soda at the gas station, Alfred was smiling in a way they hadn't seen before. He didn't seem as obnoxious, for some reason.

"See ya tomorrow," they yelled as he rode away.

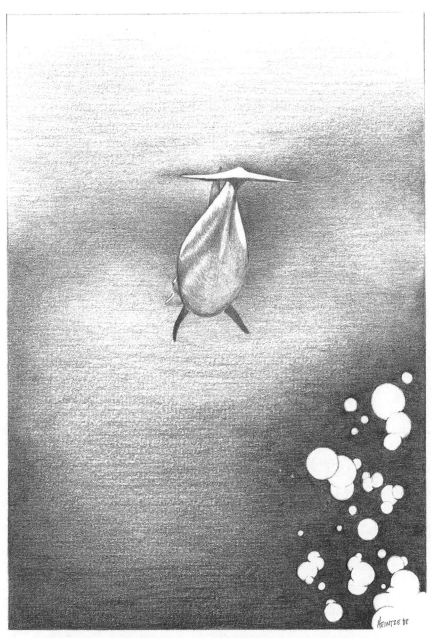

*Farther and farther they went, Cloud always fifteen or
twenty feet ahead, acting as their scout . . .*

30

CHAPTER FIVE

"Friend!"

The next morning was Saturday. Mr. Anderson had a standing tee time at the golf course for 8:15, so the boys still had "good-old-dad" to take them to the beach.

"Look, Billy. No dead fish! They must have scooped them all up yesterday . . . and no brown foam!"

"Yeah, but look at all the weekenders!"

"Aw, so what? They won't be where *we're going,* Shelton!"

Mr. Anderson nudged Shawn. "Now, are you sure you don't want to come hit some golf balls with me?"

"We're sure, Dad." Shawn rolled his eyes, glancing at Billy. "It's Spanish galleons we're after . . . right?"

"Right! And gold doubloons, and bars of silver . . ."

"Oh, come on, Shelton! The sooner we get out there, the sooner we find the treasure!"

"Treasure . . . did I hear someone say treasure?" Billy giggled, following Shawn around to the tailgate.

"What about your new friend?" Mr. Anderson smiled. "Isn't Alfred going with you?"

"He's not a certified diver, Dad. He's just a snorkler."

"He'll show up sooner or later," Billy laughed. "He always does."

"All right . . . you guys be safe. And watch your air. I'll see you later this afternoon."

* * *

The water wasn't as clear as it had been the day before. Choppy waves were breaking on all three sandbars, and little glumps of tar washed in with the shorebreak.

Weaving their way through the fishermen and screaming children thrashing around in the surf, Shawn and Billy finally reached the third sandbar and stopped to rest. Chest-high waves slapped their thirteen-year-old bodies around like corks.

Shawn sighted the old pier, checked his pressure gauge, and pointed to their right. "I think it's . . . out there. Let's go."

Billy nodded his agreement and followed, holding fast to the shovel and grinning through his face mask.

Shawn was right. They went straight to the underwater balloon buoy, still securely fastened to the piece of wood. But only a couple of feet of Billy's ship rail was visible. It looked like they hadn't done any digging at all.

Billy shook his arms and head in disgust. The ocean floor was reclaiming its secret and there wasn't much they could do about it.

"Oh *gr-e-a-t*," Shawn grumbled to himself. "I was afraid something like this might happen."

Billy didn't waste any time. He had the plastic bags out — one already full — by the time Shawn joined him. The sandy bottom shifted and filled in any progress Billy made, but he kept on digging, persistent and determined not to lose his ship rail.

This isn't going to work, Shawn thought. *We might as well just make sure the buoy is tied well, and —*

Click-click-click-click . . . wheeeeoooouu . . . click-click-click-click . . . wheeeeoooouu . . . click-click-click-click! Cloud had sounded his arrival.

Oh, hi fella! You kind of scared me a little, thought Shawn.

Cloud swam past Shawn and straight to Billy, nudging the shovel and whistling. Billy stopped digging, shrugged his shoulders, and began stroking the dolphin's side.

Shawn looked at his watch. They'd been down less than ten minutes, so he figured they had at least fifty minutes worth of air left in their tanks. "Half of fifty is twenty-five, so we can follow him that long, at least."

Suddenly, Cloud bolted, swam out fifteen or twenty feet, and started his beckoning melody.

Okay, Cloud. We're going with you today.

Billy stuck the shovel in the sand next to the ship rail and shook his head. This just wasn't a good day for treasure hunting — or was it?

"Come on, Billy," Shawn gestured. "It's useless. Let's see what Cloud has up his sleeve."

Softening his melody as they approached, Cloud swam out another twenty feet or so and turned, glancing back just long enough to make sure they were following before continuing on. His whistling diminished to a constant muttering of sonar clicks and low barks as the dolphin led them farther out.

Shawn checked his compass. Cloud was leading them due east. *Amazing,* he thought. *He's following a perfectly true course. He must have a built-in compass.*

They passed through a school of the largest redfish either of them had ever seen, and over a group of small hammerhead sharks skimming the bottom. But there was no shipwreck. Farther and farther they went, Cloud always fifteen or twenty feet ahead. He was acting as their scout, leading the way.

Shawn glanced at his watch. Fifteen minutes had passed and the dolphin hadn't slowed or deviated from his easterly course. The water was clearer and less turbulent now. He quickened his pace to catch up with Cloud, and gestured for Billy to follow. *Come on, Cloud . . . We're running out of time. Where are we going?*

Cloud barked a few notes and adjusted his pace, keeping the boys a comfortable distance behind, but always maintaining his lead. Then, veering slightly downward, the dolphin followed the gradual slope of the ocean floor, deeper and deeper. Shawn looked at his

A pale, pink light emanated from both of the domes.

depth gauge. *Still only forty feet ... no problem,* he thought, glancing at his watch. Twenty minutes and nothing in sight, except a school of amber-jack that had joined the procession behind the boys. *Now what?* he thought. *This is too much. Why are they following us?*

Just then, he felt Billy tapping on his shoulder and pulling his arm. Shawn turned to see his friend frantically motioning for him to look down to his right. He looked—but didn't believe what he saw.

The ocean floor had suddenly dropped off into a deep canyon. As they followed the dolphin deeper and deeper, the water felt cooler and gradually became clear enough to see a huge ...

What is it? Shawn wondered. *Naw ... it couldn't be ... It is! It's a huge glass dome!* He looked at Billy and gestured as if to say, "What in the world is that thing doing down here?" Billy just shook his head and turned back toward the dome, following the dolphin.

As they drew nearer, another dome came into view, this one much smaller and sitting a good distance behind the larger one. A shiny metal cylinder connected the two structures.

This is too much! Shawn sighed into his mask.

A pale, pink light emanated from both of the domes, and Shawn could faintly see familiar forms inside. They looked like ... trees?

Around the bottom edge of the larger dome was a wide band of metal with hundreds of oval portholes, some glowing with colored lights, others flashing on and off brightly, like strobes.

The dolphin's pace hadn't changed. He was still swimming directly toward the domes, but the boys were lagging behind.

Outrageous, Shawn said to himself. The sheer immensity of the dome was overwhelming. Now he could see buildings inside, and trees that reached to the topmost limits of the glass hemisphere.

Cloud proceeded to a small, gold-colored plaque near

the base of the huge dome and bumped into it with his nose. A ring of tiny red lights began flashing, and a tunnel suddenly appeared inside the lights. Cloud glanced back at the boys, and, in the wink of an eye, was gone.

Shawn looked to his friend for a little encouragement. Billy was shaking his head no and signing "thumbs down." They spent the next few seconds, which seemed like days, staring at each other, the dome, and the tunnel where Cloud had disappeared. Then they heard it. At first it was a soft clicking. As it intensified, louder and louder, suddenly *Whish!* — Cloud emerged, twirling around and around and then back into the tunnel. He returned seconds later, repeating the same beckoning melody he had used before.

Oh no, you don't! Shawn held the palms of his hands up to the dolphin and shook his head. *I'm not following you in there. What* is *it, anyway . . . some kind of research station . . . or astronaut training lab?*

Cloud barked a few low notes, nodded his head from side to side, and slipped back into the tunnel.

The boys just hung there, shrugging their shoulders and staring at the hole in the metal band.

Shawn pondered. There could be scientists or researchers inside. They could be involved in some new experiment with dolphins. He heard it again. Cloud was coming back. *What could it hurt?* Shawn thought. He gestured for Billy to go inside with him.

Billy's first reaction to Shawn's idea was to back off and shake his head. But when Cloud returned, and Shawn moved toward the tunnel entrance, he gave in.

Okay, fella, lead the way — we'll follow, Shawn gestured.

The tunnel, dimly lit by thin tubes that glowed pink, wasn't very long. Shawn could already see a bright hole of light ahead, but the water was different. Somehow, it felt cleaner, or thinner, and cooler. They seemed to slip right through it, with much less effort. Then, quick as a wink, they shot out of the tunnel and into what looked like a small pond.

Through the clear water, Shawn could see the overhanging branches of trees — and the dolphin, treading water near the bank. *What have we gotten ourselves into this time?* he thought, turning to his friend.

Billy was waving his hands through the water, feeling the gliding sensation and nodding his head. When he noticed Shawn looking at him, he pointed to the surface and shrugged his shoulders.

Well, I guess so, Shelton. I mean — we came this far, didn't we? A tinge of nervous electricity shot through Shawn's spine as he began his ascent. What *had* they gotten themselves into?

Milliseconds later, their heads popped through the surface and into a warm, brightly lit area surrounded by trees of all kinds, bushes, grass, and flowers.

Billy pulled off his face mask and mouthpiece, took a deep breath, and sighed. "Well, I know one thing, Toto. This isn't Kansas."

The boys began laughing nervously, giggling and gasping, until, from behind, they heard something that made them stop cold with mouths agape.

"Friend," they heard a strange voice say. It sounded like a cross between a computerized robot and an electric can opener.

The boys slowly pivoted around, peeking over their shoulders as they turned. There it was . . . standing on the bank . . . talking to the dolphin. Most of what it said sounded like mechanized gibberish, but from time to time an English word would surface . . . like water, food, and air.

Shawn looked at Billy. "What is it?"

"Are you kidding? How should I know? Looks pretty strange to me."

Cloud turned abruptly toward the boys and sounded, "Friend . . . come!"

"Did you hear that?" Billy blurted.

"Yeah, I heard it," Shawn replied. "Friend," he said to

the dolphin, and then he looked at the alien figure standing a few feet away. "Friend?" Shawn said to him. "I hope you're a friend too—or we're in big trouble."

The figure on the bank resembled an extremely thin young human — about the same height as the boys — with an incredibly large head and eyes. The eyes were enormous, but not scary or frightening. In fact, there was an eerie human quality about them—curious, but a little apprehensive. He looked as surprised as they were.

"Friend! Friend!" the dolphin broke in, splashing a thin spray of water on the alien.

"Friend," the alien said, holding up his left arm. His hands were long and thin with three long fingers. The fingers were almost identical to Shawn's — only longer, with thick, black nubs instead of fingernails. The greenish-brown color of his skin and the complete lack of hair made him look more reptilian than anything.

"Unreal!" Billy mumbled. "He's talking to us. I don't understand what he's saying, but he looks friendly—in a weird sort of way. What do you think?"

Shawn raised his left hand and repeated, "Friend. Yes—we're friends. Are you a friend?"

The alien answered in his peculiar language. The boys didn't understand most of it, but they did react when he said "Come," and gestured for them to come out onto the bank.

Shawn had already decided to go for it. He looked at Billy, winked, and moved slowly toward the grassy edge of the pond.

The alien walked over, his long, skinny feet springing through the thick, wet grass, and extended his right arm. He jabbered something, ending with the English word "rest."

Shawn tossed his mask and fins onto the grass and reached up to accept the alien's help. The alien grasped his wrist, and Shawn his, and hoisted the human out of the water effortlessly—as if Shawn didn't weigh anything.

"Hey, take it easy!" Shawn grimaced, shaking his

hand free. "What a grip. His skin is soft but his grip sure isn't." He turned to Billy. "Come on — I'll help you up."

"No thanks, I mean, one of us should stay in the water, don't you think? In case . . . I don't wanna come out just yet, okay?"

"Come on, Shelton. You can —" His sentence stopped short when he felt the alien's hand on his feet. "Now what are you doing . . . uh, friend? I know they don't look like yours, but they're my feet, okay? Nice alien."

"Be ready to grab your stuff and jump back in, Shawn. You never know — he might turn on you any minute."

Then the alien stood up and felt Shawn's air tank, and behind Shawn's ears. "Okay, guy, cool it, will you? You're making me nervous."

"Shawn, be careful! He's staring at the back of your head!"

The pupils in the alien's huge eyes were zooming in and out, focusing on Shawn's sun-bleached hair. One second they were open wide, the next, closed down to a pinpoint.

Shawn looked straight ahead and stood perfectly still as the alien's long, thin fingers ran through his wet hair and down his shoulder and arm. It was strange, to say the least. Shawn couldn't decide whether or not he was scared. Most people would be — Billy obviously was. But being near the alien wasn't frightening at all. In fact, his skin felt soothing and seemed to be giving off some kind of relaxing, comforting energy. Shawn looked into his big peepers and nodded. He couldn't help but smile. What was it that made him feel so at ease with this alien? Why was he being so brave, so willing to jump out of the pond with this creature from who knows where? It sure didn't look like anyone from earth.

"Where are you from?" Shawn probed. "Do you understand what I'm saying? Are you from this planet?"

This started the alien, who appeared equally as curious as Shawn, into a rapid, mechanical-sounding gibberish, punctuated with an occasional English word.

When he finished, Shawn could only smile and shrug his shoulders. "Sorry, guy. It's all Greek to me."

At that instant, the alien pivoted sharply and cocked his head to one side, as if he was listening for something.

Shawn looked through the bushes and trees, straining to see, or hear, whatever it was that the alien had heard. Just past the tree growth, he could see a white, cube-shaped building with a glass pyramid roof. "What's up, friend? Is there something we should know?" Then he heard it. Several alien voices, chattering and laughing, over by the building somewhere.

Standing up slowly, and moving with the stealth of an alley cat, the alien turned back to Shawn, touched his shoulder, and said, "Friend—dna!"

"What? I get the friend part, but . . ."

Now the alien was showing some emotion. He repeated, "Dna!"—this time forcefully—and pointed to the pond. *"Dna—jkewdaab!"* he persisted.

"I think he's telling you to go, Shawn. Someone must be coming. Come on, grab your stuff!"

Cloud clicked and barked excitedly, nodding his head and slapping the water with his fins.

"Yeah, I think you're right. Here, catch." He threw his face mask to Billy, slipped on his fins in record time, and slid into the pond.

Billy already had his mask and mouthpiece in place by the time Shawn got to him. Shawn grabbed his mask, turned toward the alien as he hurriedly pulled it over his eyes, and waved goodbye. *We'll be back, friend,* he thought, sinking below the surface. The last thing he saw was the alien waving with his left hand, pointing toward the tunnel with his right.

Cloud and Billy disappeared into the dimly lit cylinder before Shawn could catch up.

Hey—wait up! Don't leave me in here! All of his bravery and confidence were gone, and the last thing he wanted, at this moment, was to be left alone in the alien's

40

dome. When he shot out the other end of the tunnel, Billy and the dolphin were waiting, Cloud still clicking and barking nervously.

Shawn checked his compass and pointed due west. Then he reset the time-band on his watch, checked his pressure gauge to confirm the amount of air left in the tanks, and was off. Billy was at his side and Cloud was a few yards ahead.

All right, fellas — let's go home, he thought, as they veered up and out of the enormous canyon, stopping just long enough for one last look at the huge structure.

The pace going back was somewhat faster than before. Hearts and legs pumped furiously as the boys followed the dolphin to shore. They had covered the same distance in two-thirds the time — with air to spare.

Shawn burst through the surface, startling a group of unsuspecting children splashing about on floats. He ripped off his mask and mouthpiece in two swift motions and took a deep breath.

Billy popped up seconds later. "Shawn! What was it? Man, we really got back fast. Who was coming anyway?" He was talking so fast, his words almost ran together.

"*Sh-h-h-h!* Not here," Shawn cautioned.

"Why? Aren't we gonna tell—"

"*Sh-h-h-h-h!*" Shawn cut him off in midsentence. "No! We'd better keep it to ourselves. Remember what happened when the adults found out about E.T.?"

"Oh, yeah . . . well, what about your dad's shovel? I left it by the ship rail."

Shawn looked at his watch. "Eleven or twelve minutes," he mumbled, panning the beach for the old pier. "*Whoa,* we missed it a little, huh?" There it was, a quarter-mile down the shoreline.

"No sweat, Shawn. We can snorkle down to the pier. Then we'll have plenty of air."

Shawn wasn't too keen on that idea. "Snorkle?" he said. "In this choppy surf? I don't know . . ."

"Oh, come on, Anderson . . . you can do it."

"Okay . . . let's go," Shawn grumbled. "These kids are driving me crazy anyway."

Cloud was nowhere to be seen. Shawn thought he probably left when he heard those kids.

Switching from snorkle to mouthpiece, Shawn submerged and headed for Billy's ship rail and the shovel. Four or five minutes later he spotted the white nylon cord waving with the currents. It was still secured fast to the wood beam, but there was no plastic bag — just an empty knot at the end of the line.

Guess I didn't tie it tight enough, Shawn thought and gestured to his friend. Billy just nodded and shrugged his shoulders as he sped past.

Shawn filled another bag with air from Billy's bubbles, cinched it tight with a couple of half-hitches, and topped it off with a stopper-hitch.

There, he thought, *that's not going to come loose.*

Billy was scraping the shovel in the sand, looking for the soup ladle, when . . . clang . . . ding . . . clang.

Great! I've found it! Billy wanted to say. But what he pulled out of the sand wasn't a soup ladle. He held it up, turned it from side to side, and shook his head.

It didn't look like much of anything to Shawn either, even when Billy handed it to him.

Just a flat piece of metal, he thought, rubbing his fingers across the square holes at each end. *But, for what?* It was only eight or ten inches long and no thicker than a hardback bookcover. Heavy, though. Not gold heavy — more like brass or bronze. Shawn shrugged and handed it back.

Billy put his new "find" into the red nylon bag tied to his waist and pointed to Shawn's watch.

Shawn gestured that Billy was right. They had better get moving. He gave the buoy line one last tug, testing his knots, and started in, shaking his head and mumbling to himself silently.

It's a good thing it wasn't gold coins or a Spanish dagger. Finding those domes out there was enough for one day. Shawn jerked back as his last thought sank in. *THE DOMES . . . AND THAT . . . ALIEN! YEAH . . . IT MUST HAVE BEEN AN ALIEN!* he thought. *WHAT ELSE COULD IT BE?*

* * *

A few minutes later they were standing on the third sandbar, smack-dab in the middle of a church youth group playing water frisbee. To say that the two boys emerging from the surf in scuba gear attracted much attention would be putting it mildly.

"What's the deal?" Billy chuckled to Shawn. "Haven't they ever seen anyone in diving gear before?"

"Sure, but probably just on T.V. But, hey — this is great! We can get a ride *easy* now!"

A lady with a station wagon and three little girls took them to Shawn's house. She even backed her car up the driveway so the boys wouldn't have to carry the gear very far.

"Thanks a lot, ma'am," Shawn said as she drove away, amidst the chattering of little voices begging her to stay longer.

"Strange, isn't it, Shawn? The way they got so excited about us."

"Not as strange as that — whatever it was — out there in that big dome!"

"What did he feel like?" Billy exploded. "Weren't you scared? I couldn't *be-l-i-e-v-e* you got out of the water!"

"Yeah, I guess I *was* scared at first. But at the same time, I felt like — well, you know how you feel just before you drop into a really big wave? You know that you might eat it, but you also know that it might be a lot of fun — maybe the best ride of your life. Well, that's how I felt. Kind of like electricity tingling all through my body. And when Cloud said "Friend," and the alien answered the same way, I just had this incredible feeling — and I went for it."

"Cloud? Why did you call the dolphin Cloud?"

"Haven't you seen the marking on his back? It looks like a little cloud." Shawn hoped that was enough to satisfy Billy's curiosity. He didn't want to have to admit that he'd kept a secret from his best friend all summer.

"Cloud, huh? Yeah, that's pretty neat — Cloud." It sounded better to him each time he said it.

"But about the alien," Shawn continued, eager to change the subject. "Don't let his size fool you — he's plenty strong. I felt like a puppet on a string when he jerked me out of the water. And his skin was real soft, like Gramma's hands."

"Soft? It looked like lizard skin! And with that ridge down the middle of his head, he looked like 'Reptile Man' to me."

"Well, whatever he or it is, we'd better keep quiet about it."

"Even with Alfred? He *did* show us *his* secret place." Billy couldn't believe what he'd just said. He was actually sticking up for Alfred.

"Yeah, Shelton. But this is bigger than any secret about World War Two planes in a dumb old hangar. Besides, we don't really know him that well yet."

"You're probably right," Billy conceded. "Hey, I almost forgot about this . . ." He reached for the red specimen bag. "I think it's brass, or maybe bronze. What do you think?"

"Take it over to the hose. I'll get a scrub brush and some soap."

"Ammonia, Shawn. See if your mom has some ammonia."

Minutes later, Shawn returned with a scrub brush in one hand, a bottle of ammonia in the other, and his mom trailing behind.

"What do you two rascals have that you need ammonia to clean?" she quizzed. "What did you find out there?"

"I don't know what it is, Mrs. Anderson," Billy replied. "It's just a piece of metal. It was by that old beam we found the other day."

"Billy thinks the wood is a ship rail from a Spanish galleon," Shawn added.

"Did I hear you say Spanish galleon?" Alfred's voice surprised them from behind the garage. "Did y'all really find a Spanish galleon?"

"Where did *you* come from?" Shawn jerked back. "How long have you been there?"

"I just walked over from my aunt's house," Alfred replied. "She lives behind you . . . over there." He dropped his bike in the grass and pointed to the yellow and white house directly behind Shawn's.

Mrs. Anderson started walking toward the back porch. "Just don't forget to put that brush and ammonia back where you found it," she called over her shoulder. "And before you make any plans for tomorrow, remember what you promised your dad."

"Oh, that's right," Shawn grumbled. "The garage."

"Hey! What about this Spanish galleon, you guys?" Alfred interrupted. "Where did you find it? What's that you have there?"

Shawn looked at Billy. Now what? Should they tell him? He thought for a minute, and then it came to him. Of course . . . it was obvious. "Well," he said, "I guess we should tell Alfred about our secret *shipwreck,* huh, Billy?" He winked and raised his eyebrows when Alfred wasn't looking. "I mean, our secret *shipwreck* is about as special as Alfred's G.I.S., don't you think?"

Billy smiled. He was catching on. "Oh, yeah," he agreed, "the *shipwreck.* I guess it's only fair." He snuck a wink back at Shawn.

"Let's go over to G.I.S., Alfred," Shawn suggested. "We'll tell you about it when we get there — so no one will overhear."

"Good idea," Billy chimed in.

"Great," Alfred agreed. "Let's go."

* * *

Less than an hour later, they were leaning their bikes against the back side of the hangar.

"*Sh-h-h-h,*" Alfred whispered. He peeked around the corner of the building, then motioned that all was clear. "It's okay," he said, "no supply boat."

"Great," Shawn piped up. "Let's check out that pier."

"Look, Anderson," Billy pointed, "more crates. But where did they come from? I don't see any roads, or tire tracks."

"Probably another boat," Alfred suggested.

"Wait a minute!" Shawn stopped dead in his tracks. "Look at that cable!"

"Yeah," Alfred replied. "It's always been there. It goes back over the dunes."

"Where to?"

"I don't know. I've never been that far back in the high dunes."

Shawn followed the cable with his eyes. "It goes all the way to the pier," he said, "to that ramp."

They climbed up the rotting steps to find a solid platform, rebuilt in places with new timbers. The wooden crates were sitting in a line, one behind the other, backed up on the ramp which slanted down and onto the pier.

"I wonder what's in these things?" Alfred said, peering through a crack in the crate nearest the railing. "It's a big metal drum. You know, an oil drum."

"You're right," Billy agreed. "What does it say? I can't see enough of it from here."

"Detergent?" Alfred said. "What do they need *that* much *detergent* for?"

"Guess those guys get pretty dirty out there on those oil rigs," Billy offered.

"Get serious, Shelton," Shawn chuckled.

Alfred was looking into each crate, laughing as he strained his eyes to see through the narrow cracks. "They *all* say detergent." He shrugged his shoulders.

46

"Hey, look at the cable," Billy pointed. "It makes a turn around that wheel, like a ski lift."

Shawn stared at the steel wire. "And look . . . only the bottom side is rusted. The top is shiny."

"*Sh-h-h-h-h,*" Alfred warned. "I hear the boat."

He was right. The supply boat was coming. They could see it now, approaching from the southeast.

"*Run for it!*" Billy yelled. He jumped off the pier in a flash, slipping in the sand as he sped toward the hangar.

Shawn and Alfred were scrambling behind. They ran around and behind the hangar, where they had left their bikes, and fell in the sand, panting.

"Do you think they saw us?" Alfred gasped.

"I sure hope not," Shawn whispered, peeking around the corner with one eye.

The supply boat pulled up to the pier and two men jumped off, just as before, but the mysterious black-bearded man in the wheelhouse didn't come out at first. When he did step out, he had binoculars in his hands.

"*Crimony!*" Shawn cringed. "He saw us! He's got field glasses, and he's looking this way. Let's get out of here — fast!"

They grabbed their bikes and started pedaling as fast as their legs would pump, to the opening in the dunes behind the hangar.

As soon as they were out of sight, Shawn skidded to a halt, dropped his bike on the sand, and crawled up the back side of the dunes. Billy and Alfred stayed on their bikes.

"What's up, Shawn?" Billy panted.

"They're looking at our bike tracks in the sand," Shawn whispered back. "Now they're looking over here."

"Let's get out of here," Billy insisted.

"Yeah, let's go, Shawn," Alfred agreed.

"Wait . . . they're going back."

"I still think we ought to get out of here," Billy urged.

"It's okay," Shawn said, motioning for them to calm down. "They're gone."

About that time the engines of the supply boat revved up and a few seconds later Shawn could see it speeding off, heading out to sea. "Wow, that was close," he mumbled.

"Something's weird about this place," Billy said, leaning his bike against Shawn's and plopping down on the soft sand. "They wouldn't have chased us if—"

"If what?" Shawn interrupted. "We're not even supposed to be *on* this island. They might be reporting us right now."

"For what?" Alfred piped up.

"For trespassing on government property! Have you forgotten that this whole island is off-limits to the public?"

Billy suddenly looked alarmed. "That's right!" he jumped up. "Come on, Shawn, let's get out of here!"

As they rode off, Alfred remembered why they had come in the first place. "Hey! What about the shipwreck? When do I get to see your shipwreck?"

Shawn and Billy skidded to a halt.

"Now wait a minute, Alfred," Shawn spoke up. "We never said we'd *show* you the ship rail. Besides, that's all it is . . . just a big piece of wood Billy thinks is part of a ship rail. That's all."

"But I showed you *my* secret place!" Alfred insisted.

"Relax, Alfred," Billy chimed in. "Tell you what . . . When we get the rail dug out enough and we're ready to bring it up on shore, we'll let you help us hide it someplace. How's that?"

"Copasetic," Alfred grinned. "Copasetic."

Billy squinched his nose. "What in the world does *that* mean?"

"I heard it on an old movie the other night. Sounds good, huh?"

"Sure it does," Billy rolled his eyes.

"It means I've got the perfect hiding place for the ship rail." Alfred raised his eyebrows, grinning like a Cheshire cat.

"Oh, yeah?" Shawn piped up. "Where?"

"The storage shed behind my aunt's garage. It's been empty for years. I hide in there when Aunt Edna wants me to help her with the dishes or mow the lawn."

Billy and Shawn exchanged glances.

"We'll have to check it out," Billy winked at Shawn.

"First we have to dig up the rail." Shawn giggled. "The way we're going, it might take the rest of the summer."

As the boys rode on, into a sudden gust of wind, they clinched their handlegrips and squinted their eyes. One of them, Alfred, was still grinning, sand or no sand. He was finally "one of the guys."

CHAPTER SIX

The Footlocker Connection

Shawn hung his dark blue Sunday suit in the closet and fell back on the bed. Puffy white clouds floated past his window. They were pristine little clouds in a powder blue sky. It was the perfect backdrop for daydreaming. He'd sure been doing a lot of that this morning . . . about the alien, the domes, the supply boat on Gull's Island, and the dolphin. Why had Cloud led them out to the domes in the first place? Was the thing they met down there an alien from another planet, or a mutation from some weird scientific experiment that went sour?

Ring-g-g-g-g! . . . Ring-g-g-g-g!

"Shawn, it's Billy," Mom called from the kitchen. "Lunch is almost ready."

Hopping off the bed and into the hallway, he snatched the phone and yelled over the banister. "Okay, Mom. I've got it." He waited for the *click* from the kitchen phone before speaking. "Hi, Billy. What's up?"

"Hey, Shawn, I was thinkin' about going to the beach, but it's so windy. Look out your window and see what the waves are like, will you?"

"You're nuts, Shelton! The surf's terrible — nothing but chop. And it's already super crowded with weekenders."

"That's what I thought. But it's so boring around here."

Shawn chuckled. "Well, *I* know what you could do."

"What?"

"Come and help us with the garage. Dad says it hasn't been cleaned out since he was in high school."

"You're kidding! That was ages ago." Billy was perking up. "You know, there *could* be some really neat junk in there."

"Right. And he wants to take everything out. He's already working on it and we haven't even had lunch yet."

"I get the message. I'll be over in a little while."

"Great! Hey, bring that piece of metal from the shipwreck. Dad wants to look at it."

"Right! See ya."

* * *

As Shawn looked into the jumbled hodgepodge that cluttered their old woodframe garage, he scratched his head. Come to think of it, he'd never even seen the back of the garage. It had always been crammed full of old furniture, his Grampa's tools, and junk from years past. From time to time, Dad had cleared a path to the workbench, but before long it filled up again with stuff they didn't use anymore but didn't want to throw away.

"The trash goes in the truck bed," Dad said, startling Shawn back to reality. "Make a stack over here for the Salvation Army."

"Okay, Dad. Where do I start?"

Mr. Anderson laughed. "*That's* a good question, isn't it?"

Hours later, the backyard looked like a second-hand store. Lawn mowers, old chairs, bicycles with flat tires, tools — all kinds of things were scattered from one fence to the other.

Shawn had just about given up on Billy when a red

blur streaked up their driveway.

"Hey! Are you going to have a garage sale?" he asked, laying his red bike on the grass.

"No," Dad chuckled. "We're just trying to make some sense out of all this." Then he turned to Shawn. "Why don't you get us all a drink, son? We need a break."

"Show him the metal!" Shawn yelled back as he ran to the kitchen.

Billy pulled a folded white towel out of his backpack and laid it on the grass. He'd shined the dark metal with his mom's silver polish, so when he unfolded the towel the sun glistened and flashed on the smooth bronze surface.

"Looks like a fancy wood brace, or maybe part of an old sea chest, Billy."

"Do you think it might be old enough to be from a Spanish galleon or something, Mr. Anderson?"

"Hard to tell. What you boys need to do is to take it over to the science museum in Corpus Christi. They'll know."

"But we wanted to keep it a secret. We kind of wanted this to be *our find*. You're the only one we've told, except Alfred."

"What?" Shawn quizzed, returning with three cold bottles of soda, hoping Billy wasn't talking about the alien, or Gull's Island.

"The shipwreck," Billy answered. "I was telling your dad that we wanted to keep the shipwreck a secret."

"Oh, yeah."

"Did you mark the spot?" Dad asked, sipping on his drink.

"We made a buoy with one of Billy's plastic bags," Shawn said, "and tied it to the wood rail."

"You strung a buoy to the surface? Son, you can't keep a secret like that. Someone'll see it."

"No, not to the surface. The cord's only a few feet long. It's totally underwater."

"Well, *that's* pretty clever, I've got to admit. But it'll never stay. You've got to remember, the ocean is always in motion, especially so close to shore."

"Boy, is that the truth," Billy agreed. "We dug out a bunch of sand, and the next day it was all filled in again."

"That's exactly what I mean," Mr. Anderson nodded.

Billy walked over to the surfboards leaning against the garage. "Are these *your* old boards?" he asked. "They sure are long," he picked one up, "and heavy! How did you surf with these things?" Unable to tuck it under his arm, he propped the long surfboard on his head and strutted across the yard.

Mr. Anderson laughed. "Yeah, they *are* a lot different from the toothpicks you guys ride." He stood up and stretched. "Take them out the next time the waves get big. You might like it."

"It's a deal! Right, Shawn?"

"Sure . . . that is, if Dad'll take them to the beach for us in the truck."

"You guys are so spoiled," Dad grumbled, walking back to the garage. "We used to carry those boards everywhere."

"We can always hitch a ride if they're too heavy," Billy suggested, propping the board next to the others.

"Yeah, you're right . . ." Shawn looked to see if his dad could hear. "Tomorrow morning," he whispered, "the domes."

"I'm ready. But I want to do a little digging first. Okay?"

"Sure, we can dig a little. But, the alien—that's what I want to see . . . the alien."

"Shawn!" his dad called. "Give me a hand with this cabinet!"

"I'll be right there, Dad. Come on, Shelton. You said you wanted to help."

*   *   *

53

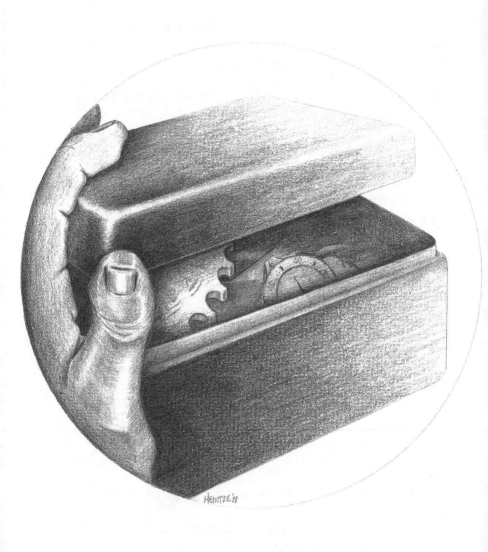

Then, prying the stiff metal lid open, he discovered ...

Shawn was more interested in daydreaming about the alien than cleaning the garage. It was all he could think about — getting back out there, seeing the alien again, asking him questions. *But how?* he pondered.

"Hey! Shawn!" a voice called from the driveway.

Billy spun around. "It's Alfred," he moaned.

"We're back here!" Shawn called back, poking Billy's arm. He was reaching into the far corner of a chest to pull out a small black box. After wiping the dust and mold from the latch, he tried to open it. "The hinges are rusted shut," he mumbled.

"Wait," Billy reached for a screwdriver. "Try this."

"What is it?" Alfred chimed in. "What's in the box?"

"Cool it," Billy scolded, nudging Alfred with his elbow.

"Here we go," Shawn interrupted, prying the stiff metal lid open. "It's a compass . . . and a diving watch . . . and what's this?" He held something up. "It looks like half of it's missing."

Mr. Anderson smiled and cocked his head a bit, as if his memory was being jogged. "That does bring back some good . . ." He paused, leaving his sentence unfinished as he stared at the shiny medallion. "By the way, have you seen that dolphin anymore?"

"We see him every time we dive," Billy nodded. "He swims along with us . . . I guess I *should* say ahead of us. And he showed us these —"

Shawn burst in before Billy could finish. "It's really neat, Dad! The dolphin shows up out of nowhere, and stays with us until we come in!" Shawn hoped that was good enough to cover up Billy's loose tongue.

"A dolphin?" Alfred broke in. "You never said anything about a dolphin."

"Well," Shawn explained. "We really didn't know if we could trust you." Changing the subject, he grabbed a deteriorated wet-suit and held it up. "Do you want this, Dad?"

"No . . . put it in the truck, footlocker and all," Dad

answered, walking out of the garage and toward the house. "I'll take this box inside."

"Hey, guys," Alfred whispered, after Mr. Anderson was out of earshot. "Want to go over to G.I.S.?"

Shawn looked at Billy. "Sure beats going to the dump with Dad," he whispered. "I've had enough of this garage business."

"Fine with me," Billy grinned. "We haven't checked out *half* of the neat old stuff over there."

"Hey, Dad!" Shawn called out, just as Mr. Anderson opened the screen door. "Is it okay if we go over to Alfred's for a while? We're almost finished here, aren't we?"

"Sure," Dad answered, staring into the metal box. "Go ahead. But be back before dark."

"Great," Shawn smiled. "Let's hit the road before he changes his mind."

* * *

Less than half an hour later, they were riding under the fenceline on Gull's Island. Alfred led them along the same path they had taken before, until they reached the flat stretch of beach just before the last set of dunes. This time, he veered left and up another path between the higher dunes. It wasn't long before they came to another opening, farther behind the hangar in the loose sand.

Alfred stopped, laid his bike on a thick clump of sea oats, and whispered. "Let's check it out."

"This is great!" Billy whispered excitedly. "I feel like a pirate or something."

"*Sh-h-h-h-h,*" Alfred warned.

They crawled to the top of the dune and looked over.

"I don't see anyone," Billy whispered.

"No supply boat," Alfred added.

"No . . . but look at the pier," Shawn said, just above a whisper.

"More crates," Billy said, standing up. "Where are they coming from? There's no road."

"Wait a minute," Alfred interrupted. "Listen . . . what's that?"

A soft whirring sound hummed through the cables suspended over their heads. It was getting closer and louder, until . . .

"*Whoa!*" Billy gasped, falling back on the sand next to Shawn. "What in the world?"

A wooden crate was slowly moving over their heads, sitting in a ski lift chair, or something very similar, propelled by a small metal box attached to the wheels which rolled along the cable. *Whir-r-r-r-r-r-r,* it sounded, as it made its way toward the pier.

"I don't get it!" Shawn said, standing up, trying to see where the crate came from.

"Look!" Alfred piped up. "The crate — it's sliding onto that ramp."

The lift chair, or whatever it was, had released the crate with enough momentum for it to slide down the ramp and into the stack of crates already there.

Whir-r-r-r-r! Another crate was approaching.

"Come on!" Shawn urged, sliding down the dune. "Let's see where they're coming from!"

"Good idea," Billy agreed.

"But," Alfred hesitated, "the brush gets really thick back there."

"Oh, come on, Alfred," Billy urged. "You can make it."

"Okay," Alfred grumbled, "but . . . you'll see."

Fifteen minutes later they reached the top of the last high dune and peered over the flat backside of Gull's Island. From that point on, half a mile or so to the intercoastal canal, no sand was visible — only thick bramble and cactus. The cables stretched across this inhospitable, stickery field to a barge dock on the canal.

"Coyotes and rattlesnakes," Billy mumbled, plopping down atop the dune. "I'm not going any farther."

"Is that a barge over there?" Shawn said, squinting his eyes.

"A barge," Alfred agreed, "and a tugboat. Too bad we

didn't bring some binoculars."

The last crate had passed overhead and they could see black smoke pouring out of the tugboat's stack when Billy stood up. "Let's go back to the hangar," he groaned. "Who cares about those crates anyway?"

"Yeah," Alfred agreed, "who cares?"

"We'd better be heading home, come to think of it," Shawn nodded. "It'll be dark soon."

CHAPTER SEVEN

Alien Cinnamon Rolls

Monday morning was still and humid. There hadn't been a breath of wind all night. The sky was a hazy gray, not a sea gull in sight. Tiny little waves lapped onto the shore as Mr. Anderson pulled up to the old pier.

"Aren't you guys getting tired of this spot?"

"No way, Dad," Shawn answered, glancing at Billy. "We've got this place wired. We use the pier as a landmark." He knew his dad would like that.

"Anyway," Billy jumped in, "tomorrow we're going out to the rigs with the Dive Club. So we've got to do enough digging for two days."

"I see," Mr. Anderson laughed. "Shipwrecks and treasure . . ." He stared out past the pier, to the horizon. "Well, you be careful . . . watch your air."

The water was so calm, it looked like a huge lake. Shawn glanced at his watch and pressure gauge as they waded out to the third sandbar.

"I guess you want to check out the ship rail before we go to the domes, huh?" he asked.

"Of course! At least for a little while. Don't you?"

"Sure, let's go for it." Shawn pulled his face mask over his eyes and slipped into the warm water. He hadn't told the whole truth. The domes — that's where he wanted to go. Right now.

Billy was more interested in the ship rail and didn't

59

waste any time. He swam directly to the site and started digging.

Dad was sure right about the underwater buoy, Shawn thought. The plastic bag was gone again — only the nylon cord remained.

Five minutes of digging seemed like hours to Shawn. He grabbed another bag of sand, shaking his head. He'd had enough of this.

Just then: *Click . . . click . . . click . . . click . . . wheeeo-o-o-o-o . . . click . . . click . . . wheeeo-o-o-o-o!* Cloud whizzed past Shawn, banked into a wide turn, and stopped next to Billy.

It's about time you showed up, fella, Shawn thought. *So . . . you go to Shelton first now, do you?*

Billy rubbed the dolphin's back, tracing the cloud-like marking with his finger.

Yeah, Shawn nodded. *That's it.*

Cloud remained almost motionless while they stroked his back and belly.

He's humming, Shawn thought, *like a baby.* He rubbed behind the dolphin's eyes. *I wonder if he lets the alien pet him like this?*

Suddenly, Cloud slipped through their hands and started swimming toward the domes, clicking and whistling.

Shawn looked at Billy. They nodded, pointed east, and both surged forward, legs pumping. *Finally — to the domes. Lead the way, Cloud.*

* * *

Fifteen minutes later, the domes were slowly coming into view. Cloud headed directly for the lights that defined the tunnel entrance, but this time he stopped and waited until they caught up before going in.

Once more, Shawn felt a change in the water as he made his way through the dimly lit cylinder. It was cooler and cleaner. He felt as if he was swimming faster, slicing through the crystal clear liquid like a razor blade.

When their heads popped through the surface, the first thing Shawn noticed was the noise — machine noise — coming from behind the buildings. He looked around, hoping to see the alien, but he was nowhere to be seen.

"What do you think?" Billy whispered.

At that instant, Cloud exploded out of the water, barking and whistling louder than ever.

"*Whoa,* fella!" Shawn jerked back "What are you trying to do? Scare the living daylights out of me?" Nervously, he turned his attention to the building closest to the pond. It was a mixture of box and pyramid shapes of all sizes. Lavender neon lights lined the edges of the windows and glass roofs. "Wait a minute — what's that?"

"What?"

"Inside that big window by the corner. I think I see someone looking out! Come on, let's move over behind the trees!"

"Why? We want him to come, don't we?" Billy asked, still in a whisper.

"Yes, we want him to come all right. But . . . I don't know. I just get a nervous feeling about the voices we heard the last time. And those noises — sounds like big machinery." Squinting his eyes, he peered through the branches. Whatever it was that he had seen in the window wasn't there now.

"Hey, Shawn," Billy's voice trembled. "Behind you!"

Looking over his shoulder, Shawn saw the skinny alien boy approaching. At least he hoped it was the same alien. A tingle of electricity shot up his spine.

The alien had something similar to a backpack in his right hand and a comforting smile on his little face.

The nervous tingle left Shawn's body the instant he made eye contact with the alien. Those big peepers looked so friendly and completely nonthreatening.

Cloud chattered and nodded his head from side to side as the alien drew near, raised his left hand, and replied in the dolphin's whistling language.

61

"I guess they understand each other," Billy whispered.

"Yeah. I sure wish I knew what they're talking about. Of course, it's got to be about us. I hope it's good stuff."

The whistling conversation stopped abruptly, and the alien motioned for the boys to come out of the water.

Without any hesitation, Shawn swam over, tossed his mask and fins onto the grassy bank, and crawled out. Billy watched as Shawn stood up to face the alien, and then it happened to *him*. The alien turned and looked into *his* eyes — deep into his eyes.

"Come on, Shelton," Shawn urged.

"I'm coming," Billy smiled, tossing his fins by Shawn's.

As soon as Billy was out of the water, the alien gestured for the boys to follow. He started up a narrow path into the wooded area.

Shawn grinned and shrugged his shoulders. "Sure, why not?" he sighed. "We came this far."

"I'm game," Billy agreed. "Let's go!"

The alien led them along a winding trail through closely spaced trees and shrubs. As they followed, Shawn noticed something odd growing on the tree bark. "Weird looking — mushrooms?" he whispered, pointing them out to Billy.

"Really! Barnacle mushrooms!"

"And the leaves, Shelton. Look at the leaves!"

"What is it?" Billy said, lowering his voice back to a whisper. "Spines . . . like on cactus?"

"They look plenty sharp to me."

Rounding the next turn, they came into a clearing under a big oak tree. It looked like a scene out of a movie, complete with a long, flat-rock table.

"*Unreal!*" Billy said, loosening his tank harness and letting it fall to the powdery soil. "We're under the ocean, but . . .

"I know! It's weird, but I'm not scared back here."

"That's what I mean," Billy continued. "This place is

exactly like the woods up around Austin. But we had to have scuba gear to get here!"

Shawn dropped his gear next to Billy's "What's he doing now?"

The alien had taken something out of his backpack that looked like stereo headphones with an attachment very similar to a microphone disc. He put them on, positioned the disc in front of his tiny mouth, and adjusted a dial on the left earpiece.

Billy nudged Shawn. "Looks like a Space Walkman."

"WHAT IS A WALKMAN?" The question blared from the disc.

The boys' jaws dropped open. Butterflies flew down their throats and into their stomachs. Neither boy could reply.

Finally, Shawn, in a shaky voice, mumbled, "Uh . . . Did you say something?"

"YES," the alien replied, fidgeting with a tiny knob on the side of the disc. "I said," he continued, lowering the volume to a pleasant tone. "What is a Walkman?"

Still shaky, Shawn quickly attempted a reply. "It's a radio . . . with headphones . . . that you carry—"

But before he could finish, Billy burst in. "Say, how is it that you can understand us all of a sudden?"

The alien cocked his head to one side, smiled, and replied. "I took this from the laboratory where the elders used to examine human specimens. It translates your language to mine through the earphones, and my language to yours through the disc."

"Wait a minute!" Billy jumped up. "What do you mean? *How* did they examine humans?"

"You just looked at them, right?" Shawn broke in. "You didn't cut into them and look at their insides or anything gruesome like that . . . did you?"

"I do not know," he answered. "That was many years ago, before I was birthed. You are the first humans I have seen, except on glass and your television."

"So, we don't have to worry about anyone catching us

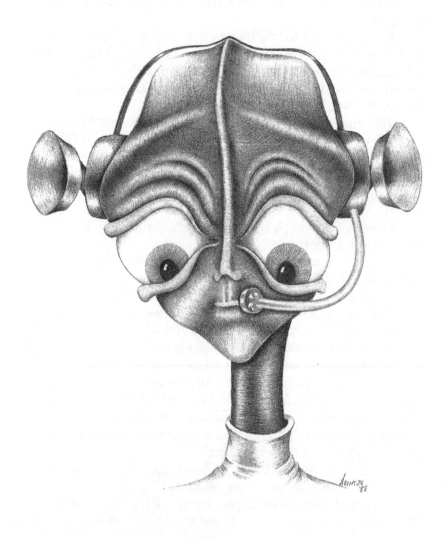

"WHAT IS A WALKMAN?" The question blared from the disc.

and examining us?" Billy burst in.

"No," the alien replied, cocking his head to the other side. "The elders are not interested in research on humans ... only plant life forms."

"What did you mean ... on glass?" Shawn quizzed.

"Glass Chronicles," the alien said, looking into Shawn's eyes. "They contain a visual historical and scientific record. Like your books, videos, and computers."

"And," Shawn continued, "did you say you watched our television?"

The alien smiled. "Your television is very ... entertaining. Although, there is much I do not understand."

"Entertaining, huh?" Billy laughed.

"Yes, your television is much different than the Chronicles from Lios." He pronounced the name "Lee-ōse."

"What's Lios?" Shawn asked.

"We are from the planet Lios, in the third orbit around the star Los. Our planet is covered mostly by water — like earth — but our water is not salty. There is no salt on Lios."

"But, why are you down here ... in a forest under the ocean?" Billy probed.

"To develop hybrids of your trees and plants. And to experiment with underwater growth in your salty oceans."

"Hybrid trees?" Shawn scratched his head. "I don't understand. What's a hybrid?"

"The elders crossbreed your trees with ours to develop a new, stronger genetic structure that will survive on Lios."

"So ... there are trees from earth on your planet?" Shawn asked.

"And plants underwater?" Billy added.

"Yes," the alien continued, "the elders have discovered that plants grown in your salty oceans produce medicines which are very effective on Lios. We have much clean water, but few trees. The tree hybrids from your planet have been essential to the reforestation of Lios."

This wasn't so hard for Shawn to believe. He remem-

65

bered studying about some medicines that can only be produced in a gravity-free environment. The Space Shuttle had launched a satellite a few years before that experimented with medicines. *If we can use medicine produced in a gravity-free environment, which can't be found on earth, why couldn't the alien's people use medicine produced in a salty environment, which can't be found on their planet? That makes sense. But why don't they have many trees?*

About that time, Billy's loud voice broke into Shawn's thoughts.

"What's your name?" Billy asked, as if he was talking to someone on the beach, not an alien from another planet. "Mine's Billy Shelton," he went on. "This is Shawn Anderson."

The alien cocked his head again and smiled, raising his left hand. "My name is Lanor." He pronounced it "Lăn-or."

"Lanor," Shawn repeated, nodding his head. Then he pointed first to Billy, repeating, "Billy!" And then to himself, "Shawn!"

"I understand," the alien said, matter of factly. "Your name is Shawn, and yours is Billy. You are both humans. My name is Lanor, and I am a Liosan."

"How long has this dome been down here?" Shawn asked, changing the subject. He hadn't intended to insult the alien.

"The bio-pod has been in this Gulf since early in your nineteenth century. But the families that live and work here stay for only twelve of our years."

At this, Shawn scratched his head and interrupted. "You said *your* years, and *our* centuries. What do you mean? Are they different?"

"They are very similar . . . only minor differences. For example, a year on earth is measured by 365 days that are twenty-four hours long. Our year is 380 days — twenty-five hours per day."

"Well, how long have *you* been down here?" Billy quizzed.

"My family is near the end of our twelfth year," he replied. "Soon I will go to Lios for the first time."

"You mean you were born in this dome?" Billy asked, glancing at Shawn, then back to the alien.

"Yes."

"So, you're twelve years old," Billy went on. "But your years are a little longer . . . so, you're really thirteen. That's incredible!"

"Incredible?" the alien questioned.

"*We're* thirteen!" Billy exclaimed, louder than he should.

About this time a rumbling in Shawn's stomach reminded him that he had skipped breakfast. The alien seemed to hear the growling, or maybe he had some way of sensing what Shawn was thinking, because he suddenly stood up and put his hand on Shawn's shoulder.

"Are you in need of food?" he asked.

"Well, I am kind of hungry." Shawn looked at Billy. "How about you?"

"I'm thirsty," Billy jumped up. "Is the water in that stream safe to drink?"

Cocking his head again, the alien reached into his backpack and produced two oversized glass test tubes, curved to fit in the hand with a little ridge that rested on the index finger. He handed one to Billy, twitched his little nose, and said, "The water will satisfy your thirst."

Then he walked over to a tall pine tree, pulled off one of the strange barnacle mushroom growths, and returned to the rock table. He took another container from the backpack, poured some dark blue liquid on the mushroom, and then went to the bark of a maple tree behind them. He scraped some brightly colored lichen onto the gooey substance, coating the top, and said, "This will satisfy your hunger."

Shawn smiled as he accepted the concoction. It

looked like an alien ice cream cone.

"The water's great!" Billy chimed in, bending over to refill his water tube. "How does *that* taste, Shawn?"

Shawn's eyes glistened as he chewed. "It tastes like a cinnamon roll with maple syrup and nuts on top."

"It looks kind of weird. Hey, want some water?" Billy grabbed the other water tube from the table and filled it for Shawn.

While they talked, Lanor prepared another mushroom and offered it to Billy.

"Thanks!" Billy accepted, eagerly. His first bite brought smiling eyes to his face too.

* * *

Shawn and Billy had finished their alien cinnamon rolls and were sitting on a rock overhanging the stream, entranced by the tiny pink fish swimming in the water, when Lanor broke the silence. "The water on your planet is not as pure as this." He cocked his head. "Although, this water originally came from your ocean . . . before the purification process."

"These fish are amazing," Shawn said. "They keep swirling around in figure-eight patterns, over and over."

Billy stood up and gazed into the tree branches above. "Do you have to *stay* in this dome for twelve years? I mean . . . it's nice in here, but . . ."

The alien cocked his head and looked into Billy's eyes. "The elders travel to Lios regularly, to take seedlings and bring back supplies. I am not permitted on the flights to Lios. But I *have* been on many trips to gather specimens."

"I thought you said you don't examine humans anymore!" Billy interrupted.

"The specimens that we gather are plants and trees," Lanor continued. "It is part of the reforestation plan." He stuffed the water tubes back into his bag and stood up. "I am also responsible for monitoring the growth of hydroplants in Sector 3."

"Do our underwater plants grow on Lios?" Shawn asked.

"Some of your saltwater plants grow on Lios. And some of our clearwater plants grow here. The hydroplants in Sector 3 are a mixture of both."

"Where is this Sector 3?" Billy broke in.

Lanor pointed behind them. "Sector 3 is near the Shuttle Dome." He picked up his backpack and walked toward the path leading back to the pond. "Come, I will take you there," he said.

CHAPTER EIGHT

Sector 3

"Wait a minute!" Billy called, as they emerged from the forest. If we go with him to Sector 3, we won't have enough air to get back!"

Shawn looked at his pressure gauge. "No problem. We still have almost forty minutes — that allows us at least fifteen. We'll be swimming slow. It'll be enough."

"Yeah, I guess," Billy mumbled. Then he turned to Lanor. "We might have to leave while we're at Sector 3. But we'll come back tomorrow — *if* you want us to!" He had completely forgotten about the trip to the rigs with Mr. Johnson.

"Yes!" Lanor replied. "Come back. I have many questions. Our time of departure is only three days from now. They are already preparing the Shuttle Dome for the flight to Lios."

"Three days?" Shawn interrupted. "You mean you're leaving earth in just three days?" He didn't want to believe it.

"Yes. It is time for a new family to take our place."

Just then, Cloud reappeared, barking and whistling. Lanor answered briefly, and then turned back to the boys.

"Come. I will take you to Sector 3." With this, he returned the translating device to his bag, stuffed it under a bush, and dove into the pond.

70

Billy looked at Shawn with a curious grin. "I guess he doesn't need scuba gear, huh?"

Shawn shrugged his shoulders. "Nothing about this guy surprises me. Can you believe it, though? He's been out here all this time, and now he's leaving in three days. What a bummer."

"Yeah, Anderson. Too bad the dolphin didn't bring us out here sooner."

"But why did he bring us here in the first place?"

"Who knows? Who cares, Shawn? Let's go see what this Sector 3 is all about."

Exiting the tunnel in single file, they veered to the right, with Shawn and Billy lagging behind the swift dolphin and alien.

They're so fast, Shawn thought, watching them circle each other, both clicking and barking constantly, looking like two children having a good time. *Seems like they've done this before. Unreal . . . he swims like Cloud.*

Lanor didn't flip his legs independently, as humans do. He kept them together, swimming more like a dolphin than a human.

Wish I could do that, Shawn thought.

Soon they were approaching the Shuttle Dome. It was clean and shiny from top to bottom, with no barnacle growth around the bottom like in the big dome. Shadows flickered inside.

Whoa, he murmured to himself. *A bunch of them . . . carrying . . . what are those?* Now Shawn could see many figures, much taller than Lanor, stacking gold boxes covered with glass pyramids. *They're little trees, hundreds of them.* He gestured for Billy to look.

Billy was already keyed in on the action inside the dome, but when Shawn turned to try to get his attention, he saw that they weren't alone. Thousands of tiny, silvery perch surrounded them, all peering into the dome, watching the aliens right along with the boys. *Incredible,* he thought, turning his attention back to one of the larger rooms below.

71

There were no ceilings, so he could see most of what was inside: computers, machines of all sorts, tools, buttons and switches on the walls, and aliens, carrying boxes of all shapes. Some contained cylinders with dark blue round things floating in a clear liquid. Another room was lined with big, comfortable chairs facing a wall covered with large TV screens and several oval viewports slanted downward. *That must be the bridge. And the room next to it looks like a . . . hospital? . . . and —*

Billy jerked Shawn's arm and pointed at the alien, who was disappearing around the edge of the dome.

Oh . . . right, Shawn gestured, and they hurried to catch up. Luckily, the dolphin returned for the two distracted humans and led them through overhanging branches of huge lavender plants with long bunches of red seed pods hanging beneath their enormous leaves.

Strange, Shawn said to himself. *I've never seen anything that big growing underwater before. It makes you feel so small.* He watched Billy follow the dolphin under one of the gigantic plants and remembered the story of Alice in Wonderland. *This must be what Alice felt like when she ate the "small" pill.*

Click . . . click . . . click . . . click . . . wheeeeo-o-o-o . . . wheeeeo-o-o, Cloud scolded, nodding for Shawn to keep up.

I'm coming, fella. Don't worry about me. He looked ahead to see Lanor pointing at — palm trees? — with bright yellow candy-cane stripes around their trunks?

Swimming nearer, he discovered white coconut-like pods under the shimmering yellow palm leaves. The coconuts were shiny and as hard as a porcelain cup.

Look at these things, Shelton, he gestured, but Billy had already ventured off. *Wait up! I'm coming. I just want to try to get one of these things loose.* He pulled and jerked, but it wouldn't budge. *Forget it,* he sighed, releasing his grip and turning to find his friend.

Billy was cautiously approaching some large blue spheres, about the size of a basketball, bobbing at the end

72

of thin black stems. They looked sort of like dark blue balloons tied to black strings.

Just then, Lanor looped around Shawn and swam toward Billy and the blue orbs. Billy was touching them now. It almost seemed as if he was warming his hands on them.

What is it? Shawn gestured as he eased up and reached out. As soon as his skin made contact with the pulsating sphere, he realized why Billy was entranced by their touch. They weren't just warm — they seemed to be giving off energy. Not energy like electricity, that shocks and hurts. This was a soothing feeling that made him feel like he was waking up with a new day's energy.

All right! This is great. I wonder what they call this stuff?

Lanor smiled and looked like he might join them when he reached over and gently pulled their hands away from the spheres.

Why did he do that? Shawn thought. *It felt so good.* He could see the same question in Billy's eyes as they stared at each other, shrugging their shoulders.

Reluctantly, they followed the alien over to an immense fern plant that had long brown vines with clusters of what appeared to be ripe grapes.

Shawn pulled one of them from the vine and squashed it between his fingers. *It is a grape,* he thought. *It has seeds inside the pulp, and a deep purple skin. But whoever heard of grapes growing in water — especially salt water?*

Then, in a flurry, eight or ten small gray fish whizzed by, just inches from his face mask, and devoured the pulp.

Billy saw what had happened and grabbed an entire bunch of grapes, squashing them between his hands and reaching for more. Instantly, more of the tiny gray fish appeared, and more, darting back and forth, grabbing every little bit of the soft pulp.

In the midst of this feeding frenzy, one grape floated free. It was still attached to a short piece of the stem and hadn't been touched by the fish.

This is like a fantasy land, *Shawn thought.*

Guess they won't eat it unless it's been broken open. Strange—you'd think their teeth would be strong enough to tear the grape skin, Billy mused.

As soon as all of the pulp was gone, the fish disappeared back into the thick fern vines, leaving only the lone grape to float to the bottom with the other discarded skins.

Shawn looked up just in time to see Billy and Lanor swim around the huge grapevine and out of sight. But before turning to follow, he stuffed the grape into a little pocket inside his waistband.

About that time, Cloud returned, clicking sternly and nodding his head.

Okay, fella. I'm coming.

The dolphin led him around the big fern plant and into a field of what looked like orange bamboo plants.

Weird, Shawn grimaced, brushing against one as they threaded their way through the dense growth. *They feel like sponges . . . with ice cold water inside.* Each time he touched one of the stalks, a cold shiver went up his spine.

When they finally emerged from the icy bamboo forest, he found Billy and Lanor hovering over acres of blue orb plants. Most of these were smaller than the sphere they had touched earlier, with extremely long stems reaching up through the depths of the canyon to the surface above.

This is like a fantasy land, Shawn thought, welcoming the feeling of warmth coming up from the thousands of blue orbs.

Lanor smiled with his tiny mouth and big eyes, pointed to one of the long thin stems, and rubbed it with the back side of his hand — always in a downward motion.

A few seconds later, Shawn realized what was happening. The stem was retracting and getting thicker. Looking up, he saw a dark blue sphere coming nearer and nearer until its stem was as big around as his wrist, and only four or five feet long.

All three of them, humans and alien alike, reached out to touch it at the same time — as if it was magnetic.

Lanor closed his big eyes and let his head fall back a little while the boys stared at each other, grinning and nodding their heads up and down. But all too soon, Lanor opened his eyes and once more gently pulled the boys' hands from the warm orb.

What's with this guy? Shawn questioned, and then reached back to touch the sphere.

Lanor shook his head from side to side and put his hand between Shawn's and the blue balloon plant.

I don't understand, Lanor. This makes me feel so good. Why can't I do it some more?

Lanor cocked his head, almost as if he was reading Shawn's mind, took them both by the hand, and slowly led them toward the perimeter of the blue orb field.

Near the edge of this vast growth, they came upon a long, glass cylinder extending out and around the icy bamboo forest. There were openings on both sides of the cylinder, allowing a current of water to flow through.

The alien swam down to the base of one of the blue sphere plants and pulled it from the sea floor. Then he tied the black stem into a knot — like a piece of rope — and shoved it into one of the openings in the cylinder.

Immediately, the blue orb was sucked down the long clear tube, around the bamboo plants, and out of sight.

Lanor continued uprooting the darker colored spheres, tying their stems into knots and stuffing them into the tube. Then he stopped, looked at the boys, and motioned for them to help.

What? Shawn thought. *I guess this is one of his chores.*

Shawn and Billy eagerly joined in, finding it easy to dislodge the plants from the sea bottom, but rather unpleasant to tie the sticky shafts into knots.

Yuk! Shawn grimaced, shoving another orb into the cylinder. *This is worse than taking out the garbage!*

After a short while, Lanor waved his arms and began

rubbing his hands in the sand, motioning for the boys to do the same.

Willingly, they heeded the alien's directions and discovered, much to their delight, that the sticky substance came off easily in the loose sand.

Strange, Shawn thought, *my hands feel so clean . . . and almost—dry?*

Cloud whistled and nodded as Lanor straightened up, pointed behind Billy, and calmly swam over their heads toward the icy bamboo forest. But this time he swam above it.

Excellent move, Shawn sighed. *I sure didn't want to have to go through* that *stuff again.*

* * *

From above, the tropical forest looked more like millions of undulating funnels, reaching skyward. A thin white haze clouded the water. It felt thicker, requiring much more effort to maintain the same pace.

What's happening? Shawn panted. *It feels like I'm pulling a boat or something!*

And then, quite uncontrollably, they all started a gradual ascent. The more Shawn tried to adjust for it, the higher he floated.

Billy was having the same problems, and soon both were fifteen or twenty feet above Lanor and Cloud, keeping up with their forward progress, but physically unable to stay at the same depth.

Noticing their predicament, Lanor veered sharply to the left just as they passed over a long, white pipe suspended horizontally above the forest, between two enormous wheels. Hundreds of white hoses which hung down from the pipe appeared to be siphoning something out of the bamboo funnels. After two or three pulses, the bamboo shafts were half the diameter and lifeless.

Looks like an irrigation system in reverse, Shawn thought, veering to the left. *Good—we're going around this stuff.* The instant they cleared the edge of the forest, swimming became easier and they dropped back down to Lanor's depth.

Sunflowers? . . . Daisies? . . . Naw, this is going too far. Flowers can't grow like that — underwater. But they *were* growing underwater, in neatly fenced-off areas, one next to the other, as far as the eye could see.

Billy wasted no time harvesting a small bunch, which he quickly stuffed into his specimen bag. Lanor didn't seem to mind, pulling a few for himself and tucking them into a slit in his jumpsuit.

While Billy and Lanor skimmed the flower gardens, something outside the fence caught Shawn's eye.

What? Is that plant moving?

On closer inspection, he saw that the slender ivy vines were growing on the backs of conch shells. The conches moved rhythmically across the bottom, long strands of ivy waving hypnotically.

It almost makes you sleepy to look at them, he thought, moving in to touch the dark green leaves.

SW-W-W-W-W-P-P-P-P! the vine hissed, wrapping itself tightly around Shawn's wrist. A horrible captured feeling turned his insides to ice, as the conch gradually sunk into the loose, almost transparent sand. He jerked as hard as he could, but the vine just seemed to tighten with each attempt. The conch sunk deeper and deeper into the sand, pulling Shawn with it.

"BILLY!" he wanted to scream. "LANOR — CLOUD — HELP!" But he knew nobody would hear. By now fear reactions had taken over, and all he could think of doing was to scream. *HELP! LANOR — CLOUD — HELP!*

It was too late. With one firm downward thrust, the conch sucked him through the thin layer of clear sand, and into a cave filled with brown, murky water.

The conch immediately loosened its grip and floated down into the depths of the cave and out of view.

Shawn frantically tried to climb back through the transparent sand, ramming, time and again, against the cave's ceiling, but to no avail. It was rock hard.

HELP! Cloud—over here!

The dolphin was swimming directly overhead, peering into the cave. Then, suddenly, he turned and swam away.

Oh, great! I bet he can't see through! Cloud! Come back! Help me get out of here! He was beginning to panic. *What if they don't even look over here?*

Pivoting around, he searched for another entrance, some way out of this trap. Why had the conch pulled him down here, anyway?

* * *

Meanwhile, back at the flower gardens, Cloud chattered nervously, pushing against Lanor's back and urging him to follow. Lanor turned abruptly, when the message finally got through, and raced across the flower beds behind the dolphin, leaving Billy in their wake.

Realizing that something wasn't quite right, Billy dropped the flowers he had just picked and rushed to follow.

Shawn's heart was pumping furiously as he poked and pushed, trying every little indentation, hoping one might be open. *There must be some way out of here!*

A shadow moved across the cave ceiling a few feet to his right. Gasping at any sign of rescue, he hurried over.

Lanor! . . . Cloud! All right, you heard me! Get me out of here! It's hot down here!

Then another shadow danced into his peripheral vision. He whipped around to see five gargantuan brown eels, slithering out of the darkness.

HURRY UP, YOU GUYS! I WANT OUT OF HERE— NOW! Shawn had never felt fear like this before. He was so scared, his arms and legs shook erratically.

Sensing the impending danger, Lanor moved into high gear. He unfastened his belt in a split second, slipped it around one ankle, and cinched it tight. Then, whistling for Cloud to assist, he put the other end of the belt into the dolphin's mouth and chattered a brief and emphatic set of instructions. The alien looked deadly serious.

Cloud clicked off a short answer through his teeth, his mouth already firmly set. He gripped the belt tightly and moved with the alien as he placed himself directly above one of the conch shell plants. Lanor looked at Cloud, whistled a note, and reached for a vine.

SW-W-W-W-W-P-P-P-P! It fastened around his arm and began pulling him down.

Shawn could see what was happening from below. He didn't understand exactly how the alien could help, but at least now there was hope. *HURRY!* he screamed in his mind. *THEY'RE ALMOST HERE!*

The eels were less than twenty feet away and closing fast, their mouths opened slightly, revealing thousands of tiny, knife-sharp teeth in each menacing cavity.

Above him, the conch was nearing the surface of the cave ceiling when — *SW-W-W-W-W-O-O-O-P* — it shot through, dragging Lanor along but stopping short at the alien's chest. No more came through.

Shawn lurched at Lanor's outstretched arm, clinging to it with both hands. *HURRY!* he pleaded. *HURRY!* He could feel the eels' eerie presence through his skin. A slight taste of bile snuck up his throat, and he felt like he was going to vomit.

Above the sand, Billy was swimming back and forth, obviously wanting to help but feeling helpless, as he watched his buddy's dramatic rescue.

Cloud was pumping his entire body, straining every muscle, determined to pull his alien and human friends to safety.

SW-W-W-W-W-O-O-O-O-S-S-S-S-H-H-H-H-P-P-P-P! Lanor and Shawn exploded through the loose sand, sending up a cloud of the sparkling, translucent granules.

Below, the eels slammed into the hard cave surface, biting at it voraciously. This was the first Billy had seen them. He jerked back nervously.

Shawn and Lanor hugged each other like longtime friends, staring into each other's eyes, until Billy tapped Shawn on the shoulder and pointed to his watch.

Oh, yeah! Shawn grinned, happy to be up there with his friends, no matter what the problem. *That's right, Shelton — the time.* His grin turned serious when he looked down at his pressure gauge — and then his watch.

Crimony! he grimaced. *We've been here too long, Billy!* He gestured that they had only fifteen minutes left.

Lanor seemed to understand their plight immediately, placing one hand on Shawn's left shoulder, the other on Billy's. *Come back soon,* he thought.

I heard that! Shawn muttered into his mouthpiece, glancing quickly at Billy. *Did you hear it?* he gestured.

Billy nodded yes, patted Lanor on the back, and gave him an enthusiastic thumbs-up.

Shawn grabbed the alien's long, thin hand. *We'll be back. Don't worry . . . we'll be back!*

Lanor nodded and then spoke to the dolphin. Cloud answered promptly and turned to lead the boys back to the domes, clicking softly.

Okay, fella, show us the way. Shawn waved to the alien, his heart still pumping, and tried another telepathic message. *Thanks, Lanor, you saved my life. I'll never forget it!*

The alien cocked his head, smiled, and then clumsily formed his long, slender fingers into the earthlings' thumbs-up sign.

All right! He does understand our thoughts, Shawn sighed, as they followed the dolphin around the bamboo, through the huge lavender plants, and past the Shuttle Dome. *Well,* he thought, turning his attention to the task at hand, *I guess we'll see how far we can get before the air runs out.* He looked at his pressure gauge, shook his head, and picked up the pace. *We'd better hurry!*

81

* * *

They made it most of the way in with the air left in their tanks, snorkeling the last quarter-mile or so. Fortunately, there had been no currents to fight or rough seas to worry about. The surface was almost as calm as it had been early that morning.

Cloud played in the surf as they crawled onto the second sandbar and stopped to catch their breath.

"Thanks, fella," Shawn said, pushing his face mask up on his forehead. "You're really *some* special dolphin. You know that, though, don't you?"

Cloud answered with several leaps and rolls, whistling happily. And then he swam over, stared into Shawn's tired eyes, and said, "Friend."

"Friend," the boys replied, reaching out to touch the dolphin. But Cloud turned and disappeared before they could get there.

"That's weird," Shawn muttered. "I guess he's had enough of humans for one day."

"Lucky for you," Billy said, "that Cloud *likes* humans. Otherwise, you'd probably still be down there with those eels."

"What are you talking about? Lanor pulled me out."

"They *both* pulled you out! Cloud was pulling on Lanor's belt. He'd slipped it around his ankle — really! They worked like a team! Good thing!"

"Well, all I know is that — somehow — I got *out* of that yukky cave!"

"How did you get down there in the first place?"

"*That* was weird too!" Shawn exclaimed, and then recounted his harrowing experience vividly.

Billy's eyes widened. "What did the eels crash into, anyway?"

"I don't know what it was. I slipped through it easy enough on the way down, but it sealed shut — harder than cement. I couldn't find any openings!" His forehead began to sweat. "And the eels! *Oooooh!* It gives me

82

goosebumps just thinking about it!"

They spent the rest of the morning and half of the afternoon remembering everything that had happened: The alien and his translating device, the gooey mushrooms, the Shuttle Dome, the blue orbs, and the rest of Lanor's strange underwater garden.

"Oh, yeah!" Billy jumped up, reaching for his red bag. "The flowers! I forgot about the flowers!"

When he pulled them out of the specimen bag, they drooped and oozed a slimy liquid all over his hand and wrist. "Yuk! *They stink!*" He ran over to the water hose, rubbing his hand on the carpet grass. "Turn on the water, Shawn. Quick!"

"Okay . . . okay! Calm down. I'll turn it on."

"Hurry, Anderson! It stinks terrible!"

The rubbing and the water took most of it off, but a rubbery brown film coated Billy's hand and forearm.

"It won't come off! Get some soap, Shawn, and that ammonia you had the other day!"

"Ammonia—again?"

"Just get it, will you? My hand is starting to feel cold —and numb!"

Shawn ran to the back porch, returning in a flash with a bar of soap in one hand and the ammonia in the other.

Billy lathered up the soap and scrubbed his hand on the grass, but none came off. "Give me the ammonia!" he demanded, frantically pouring it over his hand.

PS-S-S-S-S-S-S-S-H-H-H, it sizzled and foamed.

Shawn grabbed the water hose and held his thumb partially over the end, so that it would spray harder. "Put your hand out here!" he yelled.

The brown foaming gook washed off easily now, but Billy poured more ammonia anyway. *"Ah-h-h,"* he sighed. "That feels much better."

Relieved, they both fell back on the wet grass, staring up into the branches of a sprawling mesquite tree.

"Aw, GOOSE GIZZARDS!" Shawn slapped his head.

83

"We completely forgot about the trip to the rigs!"

"Oh, that's right! Tomorrow morning!"

"What are we going to do?"

"Well, we really don't have any choice," Billy sighed. "We can't let Mr. Johnson down, after all he's done for us . . . can we?"

"No. We told him we'd help with the light bar. We can't back out now. I guess we'll just have to wait 'til Wednesday to see Lanor again."

They lay there for at least half an hour, staring through the branches with blank expressions.

"Hey! I have an idea!" Billy suddenly hopped up, a bit of excitement back in his voice. "I know what we can do!"

"What?" Shawn mumbled.

"Let's give Lanor something to take back to Lios. What do you think?"

"Like what?" Shawn quizzed, perking up at the idea.

"Oh . . . I don't know. A football, or a baseball glove, or maybe a comic book or two."

"Yeah! I think you've got something there! I have an old comic book about baseball heroes, famous plays, rules of the game . . . you know, stuff like that. We could put it in one of your plastic bags, with a baseball. They wouldn't get wet if we sealed it real tight."

"And maybe a few baseball cards," Billy added. "I'll pick out some of the ones I have doubles of." He sprang to his feet and grabbed his bike. His hand was back to normal now. "I'll bring the ball too. Say, about tomorrow — your dad *will* give us a ride to the docks, won't he?"

"I'm sure he will," Shawn answered. "See ya in the morning!" he yelled back over his shoulder, hurrying upstairs to the closet where his comic book collection was stored.

"This'll be perfect . . . if I can just find it." His eyes lit up when he finally came to it, deep in the stack. "Here it is," he mumbled, flipping through the pages. "I wonder what Lanor will think of baseball?"

Just then, he felt something wet and gooey oozing from his swimsuit pocket. "The grape!" he winced, digging it out with his finger. The purple liquid felt cold and gritty as he rubbed it between his thumb and fingers. "It smells sweet," he mumbled to himself, cautiously tasting it with the tip of his tongue. *"Ooooh!"* his head jerked back. "That's almost *too* sweet!" He ran to the bathroom to rinse his mouth with water. *"Yuk!"* he grumbled. "The world's worst grapes — fit only for fish and aliens!"

CHAPTER NINE

The Rigs

Tuesday morning brought dark, overcast skies and a slight easterly breeze. Mr. Johnson's converted deep-sea fishing boat, *Bottom-Time,* cut through the smooth water with almost no resistance. The air was cool and a light drizzle was falling when Billy climbed the slippery ladder to the flying bridge.

"Hey, it's better up here under the canopy," he said, in his usual loud tone. "The raindrops feel like BBs hitting your skin."

Bob, who had been Mr. Johnson's assistant diving instructor for years, was at the helm, and Shawn was leaning back in the captain's chair with his feet propped up.

"Don't worry about the rain," Bob reassured them. "It's only mornin' showers. We'll be through them and in the sun before you know it."

"How far out are we going today, Bob?" Billy asked, climbing into the chair next to Shawn.

"Eighteen miles," Bob answered. "We'll be there in thirty — maybe forty — minutes."

Shawn wasn't paying much attention to the conversation. He could hear them talking but just couldn't seem to pull himself out of his daydream. *How can they have been down there for so long without someone finding them?* he thought. *But then, we didn't really find them, either. If Cloud hadn't taken us to the domes to meet Lanor, we would never have thought to go diving there. It is kind of an odd situation anyway. A deep canyon, a mile or two from shore. I wonder . . .* He quickly turned his gaze toward Bob. *I wonder if Bob knows about any canyons around here?*

"Hey, Bob," he asked. "What's the ocean floor like around here? Are there any reefs or trenches that you know of?" He winked at Billy. "Or canyons maybe?"

"Well," Bob paused, thought a minute, and replied. "There's a man-made reef of old Liberty Ships about eight miles out, and another one made from old wrecked cars up the coast a'ways." He pulled his hat down a little and rubbed his chin. "I've never heard of any canyons in these parts, though. Why? Are you thinkin' about some deep divin'?"

"No . . . just wondering," Shawn answered. "Just wondering."

It was almost 10:00 A.M. when Bob pulled up next to an inactive oil rig, towering over the *Bottom-Time.* Shawn and Billy joined Mr. Johnson and the other Dive Club members on the main deck, where they were already breaking out diving gear and air tanks.

Mr. Johnson was fidgeting with the chains to the diving platform. "Barnacles," he muttered. "Whoever stowed these chains needs a lesson—"

"Can I help?" Shawn offered.

"Thanks, Shawn," he laughed. "Just tryin' to figure out this 'creative packing.' There—that ought to do it. Now, if you'll get on the other end and help me lower this over the side." He was still laughing. "Let's do it together. Ready?"

Mr. Johnson was the sort of man you always wanted to please. But if you *did* do something wrong, he always managed to find something humorous about it. Then he'd show you the correct way—with a smile.

"You and Billy need to stay close to me on this dive," he said, securing his end of the heavy platform. "Some of

87

the men are takin' spearguns. I don't want any accidents."

"Sure thing, Mr. J.," Shawn replied, as Billy walked up, carrying his gear. "Did you hear that?"

"That's fine with me. How deep are we going?"

"Oh, probably between sixty and eighty feet. How's your depth gauge workin'?"

"Fine, sir," Shawn answered, smiling and nodding. "Everything's working fine. We've just been diving from the beach — by the old pier."

"Is that right?" the burly old man said, lifting his eyebrows. "Your dad liked that area too."

"Yeah, we found a shipwreck . . . I think," Billy interrupted.

"So, you mean old Treasure Map finally found a shipwreck, huh?"

"It's just a big piece of wood sticking out of the sand, with round holes in it," Shawn added.

"Belaying-pin holes," Billy insisted. "It's part of a deck rail to an old Spanish galleon. I just know it is!"

"Well," Mr. Johnson laughed, stroking his sunbleached mustache. "If it really *is* an old Spanish ship, you'd better keep it to yourself."

"We've only told you — and my dad. Right, Shelton?"

"And Alfred," Billy moaned.

"Okay, boys. It's time we checked out *this* old rig. Maybe it's an old Spanish rig, huh?" he chuckled.

The huge pipes of the rig's supporting structure loomed ominously over the divers as they meandered their way through, descending farther and farther into the darkness. Light bars flashed on, ears popped, and hearts fluttered as they dropped deeper and deeper. They passed schools of angelfish, sergeant-major fish, jackfish, and, oddly enough, grouper — big black grouper, rogues which always swam alone, close to the barnacle growth.

That's strange, Shawn thought. *We catch grouper off the jetties. I didn't think they hung out in deep water.* He aimed his light bar at one of the ugly fish. Mr. Johnson

88

cued in quickly and clicked off a few shots. *But,* his thoughts reeled on, *I guess, if you think about it, this is a reef to them —just another man-made reef, covered with algae and barnacles.*

Billy tapped on his shoulder. He was pointing below. One of the divers was photographing a school of red snapper, as his buddy speared one. The instant the spear hit home, the rest of the school darted away — all in one motion.

Shawn looked at his depth gauge as they continued their descent: sixty feet. It felt strange to him, like something heavy was pushing down on his head. Seventy feet . . . eighty feet . . . the water was getting colder.

Suddenly, Mr. Johnson pulled up and veered to the left. There, hanging perfectly still in the water, was another enormous grouper, at least ten feet long. As they maneuvered nearer, the gigantic fish remained motionless, seemingly frozen in the lights.

In a moment of courage, Billy swam slowly and cautiously toward the lethargic giant — closer and closer, until he could touch it. But he didn't. Instead, he looked back at Mr. Johnson and nodded.

What in the world is he doing? Shawn thought, keeping his light trained on Billy and the huge fish.

Mr. Johnson clicked off shot after shot, moving around for different angles, until the grouper, tired of these intruders, silently moved away, into the darkness.

When Billy returned, the old man gave him a hearty thumbs-up and gestured that it was time for them to start their ascent.

* * *

Everyone was back on board and accounted for, relaxing with cold drinks and sandwiches, as Bob started the engines and headed for shore.

Shawn and Billy were, once again, making themselves comfortable on the flying bridge, when Mr. John-

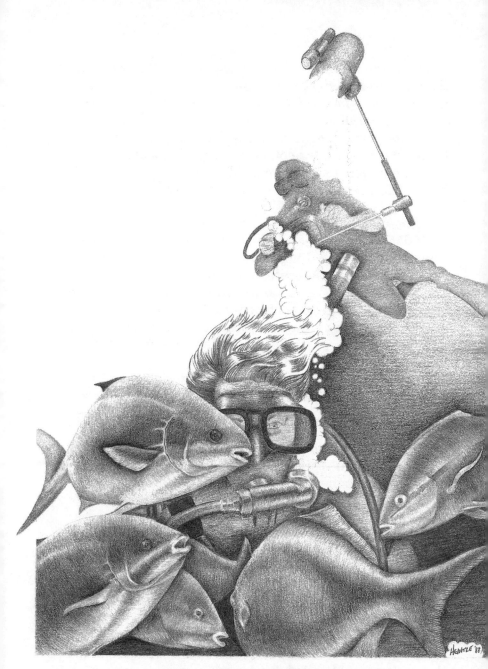

What in the world is he doing? *Shawn thought.*

son climbed the ladder. "Nice and shady up here, isn't it?" he said.

Realizing that he was in the captain's chair, Shawn quickly moved to a chair on the other side, next to Billy. "Hey — by the way. What was that all about, when you swam up to the grouper? Are you nuts or something?"

"Good work, Billy," Mr. Johnson broke in. "You got over there just in time."

"I still don't get it," Shawn said, shaking his head.

"Well," Billy answered. "I remember watching a TV show about whales, one of those Jacques Cousteau specials. Anyway, I really didn't realize how big the whales were until one of the divers swam up close to one. So, I figured the pictures wouldn't really show his size unless there was something to compare him with." He smiled and took a drink of cold soda, obviously pleased with himself.

"Those are goin' to make great pictures," the old man agreed. "Maybe we'll send them off to one of the divin' magazines."

"Pretty good," Shawn conceded, a little envious that he hadn't thought of it. "Pretty good."

Mr. Johnson eased into his cushioned chair and sighed. "I must be gettin' old," he chuckled, opening a small compartment next to his chair. He pulled out his old briarwood pipe and a brown leather pouch. "Have you boys ever seen a grouper that big before?"

"Are you kiddin'?" Billy laughed.

"Well, neither have I. Never that big. That fellow's been around for a long time, I expect." He packed the pipe with tobacco and rummaged around for his lighter.

Shawn was tired of talking about the grouper and how clever Billy had been. "Say, Mr. J.," he said. "You said something earlier about my dad liking that area by the old pier. What did you mean?"

"Well," the old man began, "your dad was a little older than you two. He used to go on all the club dives. He was always around — eager to help any way he could —

91

just to be able to go with us." He paused a moment, as if he was remembering a particular day. "One time," he continued, "the club members had voted to make a sweep-dive, just off the coast. We all spread out, tryin' to keep the divers to either side in view. The boat was goin' to pick us up at the end of the sweep."

He stopped for a minute to light his pipe. "Well, before we knew it, some currents hit us, stronger than any I've ever felt. Most of us got to the surface and into the boat, but your dad and two other men were nowhere to be seen. We searched that area, ten minutes or so, and came upon one of the other men. But your dad and one other young man were still missin'. I called the Coast Guard, and within five minutes or so two helicopters were searchin' the area with us."

He leaned back and puffed on his pipe a few times before going on. "We looked and they looked for well over an hour, but still no sign of your dad and the other fella — Jimmy was his name. The Coast Guard cutter and two smaller boats were helpin' with the search by then. Some of the divers wanted to go back in the water to look for them, but I was afraid to let anyone go back into the currents."

He tapped some of the ashes over the side and relit the pipe. "Then," he went on, "after almost two hours, we got a radio message from one of the helicopters. The two of them had just crawled out of the surf next to the old pier. Only it wasn't old then. It reached much farther out into the water. Anyway, there they were, safe and sound."

"Incredible," Shawn broke in. "Did they have two air tanks or something? I mean, how could they stay down so long?"

"You know, I've always wondered about that myself," he answered, relighting his pipe. "They each had one tank. We'd been down at least fifteen minutes when the currents hit us. And yet, when they turned their tanks in back at the shop, they both had over five hundred pounds of pressure left."

92

"Well," Shawn interrupted. "What did they say? How did they do it?"

"Said they snorkled — to save air. But seems to me the helicopters would've seen them." He sat back, puffing on his pipe and scratching his head. "All I know is that those two became best friends. They dove in that same area, next to the pier, the rest of the summer."

"You mean they went in from the beach? Like we do?" Billy asked.

"That's right. Most afternoons they'd show up just long enough to trade their empty tanks for full ones. Said they were watchin' dolphins. They didn't sign up for any other trips with us that summer." He tapped the ashes over the side and returned his pipe to the compartment.

"I've seen pictures of Dad and Jimmy on surfing trips to Mexico," Shawn said, looking a little puzzled. "But he never told me this story."

"Ask him about it sometime, son. I'm sure he'll tell you all about it."

"They could've snorkled," Billy interrupted. "We've done it before — a long way. Right, Shawn?"

Shawn smiled. "Yeah, we've done it." And then he shifted into "high-daydream." *I hope Lanor doesn't think we've forgotten about him,* he thought, staring at the horizon.

* * *

Back at Shawn's house, Alfred was knocking at the front door.

"Hi, Mrs. Anderson," he began. "I know Shawn isn't here right now ... I mean, I know he's on a diving trip. But I just wondered if I could leave this note for him."

Mrs. Anderson raised her eyebrows. "A note? Why don't you just come back in a few hours?"

"Well, you see ... we're playing this ... sort of ... game. And this is his clue for this afternoon."

"Clue, huh?" she said, taking the envelope, sealed

and addressed to Shawn and Billy. "Okay, Alfred. I'll give it to him when he gets home."

"Thanks, Mrs. Anderson. Well, I guess I'll be going. So long."

Hours later, Shawn opened the note.

"G.I.S.," he read aloud as Billy peered over his shoulder. "IMPORTANT . . . SEE YOU THERE, ALFRED. P.S. BRING FLASHLIGHTS."

Billy laughed. "Bring flashlights? Now what?"

"He probably just wants to crawl inside the back of one of those planes."

At that, Billy stopped laughing. "Yeah, no telling what he's found."

"I'm game."

"Me too!"

"All right," Shawn mumbled, walking through the kitchen to the back porch. "There's a flashlight on the shelf out here," he grabbed it, "and one in the cabinet under the sink."

*   *   *

Alfred's bike was leaning against the backside of the hangar when the boys arrived at G.I.S.

"Look, Shawn . . . no crates!"

"Good, I can do without old Blackbeard today."

Billy slid between the broken hinges, and Shawn followed.

"Hey, Alfred!" Billy yelled. "It's me, and Shawn!"

"*Ah-h-h-h!*" *Bam! Bam!* "*Ouch,* that thing has got to go!" Alfred groaned, rubbing his head. He'd just banged it hard, and was crawling out from behind two dismantled airplane wings leaning against the radio shack in the far corner of the hangar.

"I'm over here," he moaned, standing up. "Did you bring the flashlights?"

"What are you doing back here?" Billy asked, flashing his light in Alfred's eyes.

"You'll see," Alfred answered, still rubbing his head.

"I was in here the other day," Shawn broke in, as he opened the radio shack door. "There's a big chart table and hundreds of charts and maps . . . and a whole wall full of radio stuff."

"But," Alfred interrupted, "look at how small the room is, compared to how big it looks like it should be from out here."

"What are you talking about?" Billy giggled.

"I don't get it," Shawn agreed.

"Stand back here," Alfred went on. "The shack is much longer than the inside of that room."

"Oh," Shawn sighed. "I see what you mean."

"And come over here," Alfred pointed behind the plane wings. "Look! Another door . . . welded shut."

"Welded shut?" Billy exclaimed, shining his light on the metal bar welded to braces on each side. A dust-covered sign on the door read: "SECURED AREA—TOP SECRET."

Billy grinned. "This looks pretty interesting."

"Looks pretty *closed* to me, Shelton."

"The door's metal too," Alfred added.

"*Aw-w-w,* there's got to be a way," Billy insisted.

"There is," Alfred smiled. "I've already been in there." He smiled even bigger. "Wait 'til you see." He got down on his hands and knees and crawled behind the huge wings leaning against the shack.

Shawn followed silently, Billy right behind him, mumbling something about secret missions and aliens.

"*Sh-h-h,*" Shawn warned, giving him a scolding glance over his shoulder.

"Look," Alfred whispered, shining his little keychain flashlight on an air vent near the floor. He'd already taken the grate off and laid a piece of cardboard over the bottom of the opening. "It's just big enough to fit through. Follow me." With that, he disappeared into the dark hole.

Billy winked at Shawn. "Another tunnel?"

Shawn smiled and winked back as he flicked his light

95

on and pushed it through the opening. "Here we go again," he sighed.

Inside the dark, musty room the smell of years past hung in the air.

"Hello," Shawn gasped, shining his flashlight on radar screens and radio equipment, charts showing the silhouettes of German and Japanese ships and planes, and a long table with tiny models of ships and planes and a map of the Gulf of Mexico painted on the surface.

"Look, Anderson," Billy pointed. "Here's where *we* are." He'd found their location on the map. There was even a little model of a hangar and airstrip.

"This looks like something out of an old war movie," Shawn sighed.

"Check *this* out," Alfred said, shining his light on a desk in the corner. "Code books . . . bunches of them."

Shawn opened the top drawer. "More books," he said. "They all have TOP SECRET stamped across the front."

Billy was still glued to the war table, repositioning the tiny aircraft carriers, destroyers, and submarines, humming to mimic the sounds of planes and artillery.

"Is this great, or what?" Alfred gloated.

"If we just had more light," Shawn mumbled to himself, shining his light around the walls covered with silhouette charts and posters, clipboards hanging in neat rows, and . . .

"Hey, hey," Shawn perked up. "A fusebox."

Above the war table, under an air vent to the radio room, was a gray metal box marked "HIGH VOLTAGE."

Shawn climbed up on the table, taking care not to step on Billy's sea battle, and examined the box.

"*Aw-w-w,* goose gizzards!" he groaned. "It has a padlock on it."

At just that instant, a rattling noise came through the air vent from the radio room on the other side of the wall.

"*Sh-h-h-h!*" Shawn whispered, peering through the dusty grates covering the vent. "Someone's trying to open the outside door."

Seconds later, the door jerked open, sunlight streaming in. A long shadow lay across the dirty floor.

"What's going on?" Billy whispered.

"Turn out your lights," Shawn warned. "Don't make a sound. There's someone at the door."

Just then, a loud, gruff voice echoed through the opening. "Get back to the boat and swab the decks! What do you think this is, a picnic?"

Shawn strained to see who it was.

"Stinkin' landlovers," the man growled as he entered the room.

Shawn recognized him instantly. So did Billy and Alfred. They'd crept up for a peek of their own.

"Wastin' time," the man grumbled, plopping down in a chair next to the radio desk. It was Blackbeard, and he didn't look very happy. He opened the bottom drawer and pushed the files aside. "Wastin' time," he repeated, pulling a half-empty bottle of whiskey out and slamming it down on the desk. He reached for a switch on the radio panel and flipped it up. Tiny red lights flashed on and a high-pitched hum resonated from one of the amplifiers.

How'd he get that to work? Shawn thought to himself, as he watched Blackbeard take a dirty, moldy glass from the drawer and wipe it with his shirttail.

"Stinkin' bargenellies," he grumbled, pouring a glassful of whiskey and gulping it down before grabbing the microphone. "Bargedock forty-two . . . come in!" he barked into the microphone. Then he repeated the same call as he poured another drink and waited for a reply.

"PIER FORTY-TWO . . . COME BACK!" the radio blared. "THIS IS BARGEDOCK FORTY-TWO CALLING PIER FORTY-TWO . . . COME BACK, PIER FORTY-TWO!"

"I hear ya," Blackbeard growled into the mike. "Where's today's load? What are ya doin' over there, takin' a holiday?" He poured another drink.

"THE CABLE IS DOWN . . . RESCHEDULE FOR

97

TOMORROW . . . ACKNOWLEDGE PIER FORTY-TWO!"

"What?" Blackbeard yelled, slamming the bottle down so hard that whiskey spurted out. "What're ya doin' over there? *Fix* the stinkin' thing."

"CABLE IS DOWN . . . RESCHEDULE FOR TO-MORROW!" the radio repeated.

Blackbeard grabbed the mike with a strangling grip. "Tomorrow!" he growled. "I've gotta pay my crew for the day. Get the stinkin' crates over here now!"

"RESCHEDULE FOR TOMORROW . . . BARGE-DOCK FORTY-TWO, SIGNING OFF!" the radio replied.

"Bargenellies," Blackbeard grumbled, switching the radio off. "I oughta go back to runnin' supplies to the rigs," he growled, grabbing the bottle and kicking the drawer shut. He slammed the door behind him on the way out.

"Man," Alfred whispered. "I sure wouldn't want to be working for him."

"I don't get it," Shawn said, flicking his light on and jumping down from the tabletop. "He said he ought to go back to running supplies to the rigs. Where's he taking those crates if he's not taking them to the rigs?"

"Who cares?" Billy muttered.

"I wonder why we didn't hear the supply boat?" Alfred broke in. "This room must be soundproof or something."

"That's right," Shawn agreed. "I hadn't even thought about that."

*　*　*

Another hour passed before their flashlight batteries played out. Shawn had managed to cut the padlock off the fusebox with a bolt cutter Alfred had found in the tool cabinets, but to no avail. All the fuses were duds.

"The planes," Billy said, as he followed Alfred out the vent opening. "Let's check out the planes."

"You guys go ahead," Shawn said. "I'll be there in a

minute." He walked into the radio room and flipped the light switch up. Nothing happened. Then he flipped the nearest radio switch. Nothing. Then another, and another. Nothing came on until he got to the one old Blackbeard had used.

"Weird," he mumbled, "why only one?" He went to the fusebox near the outside door. "So . . . that's why." All of the fuses except one looked as old as the ones in the war room. He unscrewed it a bit and the radio amplifier turned off. *That's it, all right,* he thought, screwing it back in. The radio hummed back on.

"Hey, Shawn!" Billy yelled from across the hangar. "Let's go get some burgers . . . Alfred's buying!"

CHAPTER TEN

The Glass Chronicles

That night Shawn didn't sleep much. At one point he had crawled out of his bedroom window and onto the roof over the front porch. The wind had turned northerly again, blowing all the clouds away. He lay back, gazing into the trillions of stars, listening to the waves breaking on the beach, his thoughts crisscrossing between what he wanted to say to Lanor, the story Mr. J. had told him about his dad, and, of course, Blackbeard.

It was the same area, he thought. *And Lanor did say the domes have been down there since the nineteenth century. Could Dad and Jimmy have ducked in to escape the currents? Did* they *meet an alien too?* He rubbed his chin. It was one of those "deep thought" rubs. *Naw,* he mumbled to himself. *And what about old Blackbeard? I wonder what he's up to?* He stopped rubbing his chin and stared ahead. *Drugs . . . that's it. I'll bet he's a drug runner.*

Just then, he heard Billy skidding his tires as he rounded the corner and turned into their driveway. Shawn whistled softly to get his attention. "I'll be down in a flash," he whispered, crawling back through the window. He quickly straightened his bedspread, grabbed the comic book, and headed down the creaky staircase, tiptoeing so he wouldn't wake his parents.

Billy was sitting on the back porch when Shawn opened the kitchen door.

"Want some toast and jelly?" Shawn asked, flicking on the porch light.

"Sure," Billy answered quickly, holding up a large plastic bag containing one well-worn baseball and a few old baseball cards.

"Great . . . the comic is on the table. Do you want orange juice or milk?"

"Juice," Billy answered, flipping through the frayed pages. "Fantastic, it's all here. He can figure it out *easy* with this book. Besides, I'll bet he's seen baseball games on TV. He *did* say he'd seen humans on television."

"Cool it," Shawn broke in, pointing upstairs. "Dad's alarm just went off."

"Right," Billy whispered. "Let's eat this out back, while we load the gear. By the way, did you ask your dad about what Mr. J. said?"

"Naw," Shawn whispered. "The way I see it, he's got his secrets . . . and we've got ours."

Billy looked back and smiled. "I'll say," he laughed. "We've got enough secrets to fill a Hardy Boys' mystery."

* * *

The wind felt even cooler when they turned onto the beach.

"Look at those waves!" Billy exploded.

"Unreal!" Shawn chimed in. "It's the offshore breeze, holding them up like winter surf!"

Mr. Anderson pulled up to the old pier and turned to the boys. "Want to take the diving gear back and get your boards? Maybe even the long ones?"

Shawn and Billy just looked at each other, puzzled.

"Such a deal," Shawn mumbled. "Absolutely the best waves of the summer, but . . ."

"But what, son? This is a perfect day to try the long boards."

Shawn glanced back and forth between the waves and Billy, scratching his head. "No, Dad . . . we'll catch some waves this afternoon. We're kind of anxious to get back to the shipwreck and do some more digging. Right, Shelton?" He hoped that was good enough to satisfy Dad.

"Yeah, I guess so," Billy answered. "I hate it when I have to make choices like this." He popped the door open and jumped out. *"Look!"* he screeched. "Dolphins!" He ran to the shorebreak and started screaming, "Oh no . . . Oh no . . . not Cloud!"

Shawn sprang out of the truck, running as fast as his legs would carry him. He could see why Billy was so upset, and it made his stomach sour. Dolphins, three of them, lying belly-up in the shorebreak, bloated and discolored.

As soon as Billy reached the first dolphin, he could see that it wasn't Cloud, and immediately ran to the next.

Shawn wanted to scream, but he couldn't. His throat was swollen, and his tongue wouldn't move. He ran past Billy to the third corpse, and rolled it over with his foot. The swelling in his throat eased up a bit when he realized that it wasn't his friend. Instantly, he turned to Billy.

"Is it?" he yelled, his voice still a little shaky.

"No!" Billy yelled back.

Mr. Anderson drove the truck down by the shore-break behind Shawn. "Come on," he yelled. "We'll drive down the beach . . . there may be more."

The boys were back in the truck in the wink of an eye.

"What's wrong with them, Dad? Why are they dead?"

"Who knows? Maybe the same thing that killed all those fish the other day."

They drove five or six miles farther, and then turned around.

"I think that was all of them," Dad said, as he started back up the beach.

"Thank God," Shawn sighed.

"But," Billy broke in, "why did God let them die?"

102

There was a pause before Mr. Anderson said, "Well, Billy, all I can say is that you can't second-guess God."

The boys just stared ahead.

Mr. Anderson drove them past the dead dolphins, all the way to the jetties, but they didn't find any more corpses. A truck from the Oceanographic Research Lab passed them on the way.

"I'll have to drop you guys off now," Mr. Anderson said. "I have to go to work sometime."

"Take us to the old pier, Dad."

"Sure you don't want to stop here?"

"No, Dad. I want to see what they're going to do about the dolphins."

"Okay, son," he said, looking out at the surf. "I hope you find *your* dolphin safe and well. See you this evening."

The men from the Research Lab didn't have any answers about the dolphins. They just said the same thing they said about the fish kill. Tests — they had to run some tests. Another truck showed up before long, and they loaded the bloated dolphins in the back with canvas stretchers.

"Let's go, Shelton."

"Yeah," Billy replied. "Let's go out to the domes."

"I hope Cloud shows up. Keep your fingers crossed."

*   *   *

Twenty minutes later, as they were dropping into the vast canyon, Cloud shot past. He was heading for the far side of the dome instead of the tunnel.

Hey, fella . . . where are you going? Shawn thought. *You didn't even say hello. Are you all right, Cloud?*

The dolphin seemed to hear Shawn's thoughts. He turned sharply and returned to the boys, clicking ever so softly, as if to say, "*Sh-h-h-h,* follow me."

When he turned back to the domes, Shawn saw why he had changed his course.

The Shuttle Dome was bright with lights inside and

103

out. Aliens, with long pink tubes that glowed and buzzed, worked around the base, while others, holding silver discs in the palms of their hands, inspected the glass.

"*Whoa,*" Shawn mumbled to himself, veering to follow the dolphin. *I guess we're going another way.* His deepest, innermost thoughts told him something must be wrong. Why would Cloud want to avoid the aliens? And then, it hit him. *He's only friends with Lanor!* Could that be it? Is that why Cloud was leading them to the opposite side of the dome? And close — very close — around the bottom ridge to the tunnel, slipping inside noiselessly. Shawn followed him in, with Billy close behind.

When, at last, they surfaced in the pond, Lanor was there to greet them with a smile and a wave. He was sitting on the bank, almost like he had expected them at that very moment, staring into their eyes with a soothing, twinkling glow. He already had the translating device in his hand, his backpack slung over his shoulder.

"Hi, Lanor," Shawn heard himself say. "Sorry we couldn't come yesterday."

The alien quickly slipped his headphones on and adjusted the voice disc. "Welcome. I am pleased that you returned. Come."

His gaze, having put them completely at ease, lured the two boys onto the soft grass and along the same winding path they had taken the other day.

"Such a strange forest," Shawn whispered to Billy. "I mean, pine trees growing right next to willows. Walnut trees next to banana and peach, and ... look ... even avocado trees."

Billy giggled quietly, whispering over his shoulder. "Yeah, looks sort of like a tree museum, huh?"

"*Sh-h-h-h,*" Shawn whispered as they came to the clearing with the flat-rock table. "Hey," he spoke up. "What's on the table?"

Two white bowls with glass lids, two test-tube glasses, and two knives with forks at the ends lay neatly on two black placemats.

"What's this?" Billy sighed.

"I thought you would have questions about the blue orbs, so I brought some for you to taste."

"You *eat them?*" Billy grimaced.

"Only after they have been prepared in the sound-wave ovens. In their natural state, in the salt water, their energy is dangerous."

"Dangerous?" Shawn quizzed.

"Anything that comes in contact with them receives a surge of energy that continues until the plant has expended its entire supply — and dies."

"So, you mean dangerous for the plants?" Shawn said, setting one of the glass lids next to the bowl.

"No — I have seen large fish succumb."

"Succumb?" Billy quizzed.

"Die."

"Oh . . . but you say it's safe now, right?"

"The blue orb is very tasty after the sound-wave preparation. It is part of our daily food source. Eat!"

Shawn had already speared one of the dark blue slices and was carefully smelling it before touching it to his tongue. "Squash?" he sighed. He was thinking of how much he hated squash, but he didn't want to be rude either — so he ate it.

"Yeah, it's squash all right," Billy agreed, winking at Shawn. "Tastes great. But, you know, we just had a big breakfast at Shawn's house. Maybe we can save it for later."

"Right," Shawn chimed in, "for later."

Once again, Billy had come through with a good line, and they didn't have to eat the yukky squash.

"Looks like a lot of action around the Shuttle Dome," Shawn quickly changed the subject. "We saw a lot of your people working outside the dome."

"Yes," Lanor replied, sounding a bit depressed. "Our departure time has been changed. "We leave tonight. All of the families."

"*All* the families?" Billy broke in. "I thought you said

105

you've been rotating families for centuries.

"Father only said ..." he paused. "The order came from Lios—everyone returns to the home planet. Most of the loading is completed." He cocked his head slightly to one side and continued. "I *do* want to go to Lios. I have only seen it on glass." He paused again. "I also regret leaving this bio-pod, and my garden, and you, my new friends. I never had a friend my size before."

"We were thinking the same thing!" Billy blurted out. "I mean, about us finding you ... just when you're leaving and all." He scratched his head. "Well, if the truth be known ... *we* didn't find you. The dolphin led us here."

"The dolphin is a good friend," Lanor grinned. "I have known him many years."

"How do you know his language?" Shawn asked.

"I studied the dolphin and whale languages on glass. The elders helped. It is very easy to learn."

"There you go again about studying glass," Billy stood up, stretching his legs. "You mean you just watch videos and *poof* you know the language?"

"No, it's not quite that simple," the alien smiled. "I practiced many long hours with the elders, *and* studied the glass chronicles."

"I still don't understand how you can store—"

"Would you like to see them?" Lanor smiled.

"Are you kidding?" Billy burst out. "Of course we'd like to see them."

"But," Shawn interrupted, "is it safe? I mean—well, the dolphin seemed to be wary of the ... people ... outside the Shuttle Dome. And I remember the first time we came here, you shuffled us away when you heard voices."

"All of the elders are working at the Shuttle Dome. We can go to my chamber. There is a glass projector and a small library of chronicles."

"Great," Shawn grinned. "Say, by the way, what's the deal with those *freezing* bamboo plants in Sector 3?"

Lanor started down another path leading off from the clearing, and talked as he walked. "The hydro-plants strain the salt out of the sea water and store it in a refrigerated state," he answered. "They are our chief source of fresh water."

"What were the white hoses doing? Sucking the water out?" Shawn asked.

"Exactly," Lanor replied, quickening his step.

Minutes later, they came upon a building, nestled under a stand of tall pine trees, identical to the one near the pond. Lanor walked up to one of the large oval windows and touched a shiny gold key to a plaque beside it. The glass immediately slid open, without a sound.

"Follow," he said, and the boys soon found themselves in a cool, comfortable-looking room.

The walls were a lavender hue with recessed areas forming shelves of different shapes and depths. Tropical plants lined the edge, and strange-looking sculptures on round pedestals were scattered about. And on the floor . . . grass?

Incredible, Shawn thought. *The floor is grass—like a putting green on a golf course. And those chairs, they look like bean bag chairs filled with water.*

Lanor walked over to an oversized, rectangular mirror and raised his left hand. The mirror slid to one side, exposing a spiral staircase, shiny like brass or even gold. He led them up the stairs to a small, octagon-shaped room with a pointed glass ceiling. Tree boughs hung over the clear roof, and the room smelled like fresh pine needles after a rain. The walls were the same soothing color, with plants growing out of built-in flower boxes and recessed shelves similar to the ones downstairs.

"This is my chamber," he said, walking over to a desk with triangular-shaped drawers.

"Fantastic!" Billy exclaimed. "This is *all right!* Mind if I sit on your bed?"

Lanor smiled and nodded.

The bed, also octagonal in shape, rippled when Billy plopped himself smack in the middle.

"Feels like a jello waterbed. Shawn, come here —

"This is a chronicle of earth's agricultural methods,"
Lanor said.

you've got to feel this!"

Shawn was staring up through the ceiling—through the pine branches—all the way to the topmost limits of the dome. "You know," he sighed, "this place really makes you feel . . . secure . . . and rested."

Lanor sat at his desk and touched one of the drawers. It glowed pink, made a soft, low-pitched hum, and zipped open, revealing several rows of small glass pyramids in dividers with colored labels. The words on the labels looked sort of like English, but they didn't make any sense to Shawn.

Billy hopped off the bed. "What's in the drawer?"

"Glass Chronicles," Lanor replied, touching a blue button on the edge of the desktop. Instantly, a panel on the wall slid open, exposing three small television screens. Then he touched a yellow button. A small brown cube slowly appeared, rising up from the back of the desktop. He took one of the pyramids and placed it on the cube. It lit up immediately with a soft twinkle as one of the TV screens above came into focus.

The boys looked at each other, jaws almost dropping to the floor, as an American farm with cows and horses and tractors beamed out at them from this alien TV.

"This is a chronicle of earth's agricultural methods," Lanor said, pressing a red light on the cube which made the image fast-forward. He stopped on a scene depicting tractors, plowing the fields. "This is what *your* planting machines look like."

Then he removed the glass and replaced it with another from the drawer. It immediately came into focus, showing a similar scene, except the soil was much darker and the sky was a deeper blue.

The boys' jaws dropped even further when a vehicle, bearing a remarkable resemblance to the earth tractor, entered the scene. However, this one was driven by a tall, lanky alien wearing loose-fitting overalls and a wide-brimmed hat.

"And this is what *our* planting machines look like,"

he continued. "As you can see, they are very much like yours, and we plant and harvest much the same way as you do on earth."

"Amazing," Billy mumbled. "But there's no exhaust smoke coming from your tractor. What kind of fuel does it run on?"

"It operates on energy produced by magnetic inversion. Chemicals are not burned on Lios for any reason. My father says that humans are spoiling the air on this planet with carbon wastes — and destroying the protective ozone layer with fluorocarbons. Irrational, he says. Humans are irrational."

"Sounds like something *my* dad would say," Shawn agreed. "He really gets burned about stuff like that—and the rain forests. He gets so upset about them cutting down the rain forests, he yells at the newsman every time there's a story about it."

"Mine too," Billy chimed in. "He always says, 'We *know* we're ruining the atmosphere, but we're just too lazy to figure out a way to stop it.'"

"But . . . what's this magnetic inversion?" Shawn broke in. "How does it work?"

Lanor replaced the chronicle with another from the drawer beneath, and fast-forwarded. He stopped on a complicated diagram of an engine, and then pressed another button, enlarging a portion of the image.

"I do not understand completely," he began. "The engine runs on the principle of 'like' magnetic poles repelling each other. The force produced when one 'like' pole repels another is somehow magnified." He pointed to the diagram on the screen. "A series of these magnets is arranged around the inside of a cylinder, with another series of magnets embedded in the shaft, which turns inside the cylinder and also turns this larger wheel . . ." He touched the button again, zooming in on another section of the diagram. ". . . And that wheel is connected to an arrangement of belts . . ." He fast-forwarded to an image of the diagram in motion. ". . . And those eventually turn the wheels."

"Clear as mud," Billy murmured.

"No — I get it!" Shawn exclaimed. "It's sort of like a camshaft in an automobile engine, only the shaft is turned by repelling magnets instead of exploding gasoline."

"Yes," the alien agreed. "No exploding gases. Nothing to spoil the air, or make loud, disturbing noises."

"I guess," Billy sighed. "But . . . if you can figure out the energy problem so well, why do you need our trees?"

"A catastrophic event happened centuries ago, severely depleting the forests. I am not old enough to study those chronicles. Father says I will learn about it when I attend the university."

"You mean — like a nuclear explosion or a meteor hitting your planet?" Shawn quizzed.

Lanor changed the glass pyramid without answering, and selected one from a drawer on the other side of the desk. "My father says that humans do not rely on reason to meet their energy needs." The glass twinkled blue, as the screen came into focus on a nuclear reactor, next to a river, obviously on earth. "He says that you have been burning chemicals and fossil-fuels for so long that you have almost exhausted the entire supply on earth." He looked at Shawn and continued. "Now you are building these potentially destructive nuclear reactors — just to produce energy."

"Hey, our parents don't want the reactors, either," Billy interrupted. "Dad's *really* steamed about that, because now our electric bills are higher, and he says the people didn't even want the plant in the first place."

Lanor raised his eyebrows and cocked his head. "I have learned, from the chronicles, that there is more energy from the sun, and the oceans, and the winds than you could ever have need for on your planet." He advanced the chronicle to another scene by a river, and zoomed in on a pipe that was emptying sludge and chemical waste directly into the water. "Father says that humans spoil

111

two of the most important things necessary for life on earth — air and water." Then he sped the image ahead to another large river, probably the Mississippi, and a water treatment plant next to it. "And then, you use other chemicals to clean the dirty water for drinking."

"You're right," Billy conceded. "I can sure see why your father says that humans are irrational. But what about the good things on earth? You know . . . like surfing, and video games . . . hamburgers, apple pie, football games, bicycles, girls, popcorn . . . and gettin' a car in a few years."

"And baseball games," Shawn added. "Have you ever seen —"

Just then, an intense, bright light flashed in the room, brighter than a hundred flashcubes going off at once.

"FATHER! WHAT ARE YOU DOING?" Lanor yelled.

Shawn and Billy were frozen stiff, like marble statues. Their gaze was fixed on the television screen, but their eyes didn't blink. Their breathing was extremely slow, and their skin was turning a pale pink.

Two adult aliens stood near the door. One bald-headed, like Lanor, and the other with long, straight hair and a noticeably feminine body shape.

"They are my friends, Father. The dolphin brought them here." And then, obviously realizing that he still had the translating device turned on, he ripped it off and dropped it in one of the drawers. From then on, all communication must have been done by mental telepathy, because no lips moved and there was no sound. Lanor sat down and nodded his head, selecting another glass chronicle, almost like nothing had happened.

Another adult alien entered the room and placed Shawn and Billy on mats that seemed to be floating in midair. He and Lanor's father then guided the boys through a door on the other side of the chamber, into an elevator shaft that took them down three levels to a room bathed in a luminescent blue-green light. A constant, high-pitched hum made the walls vibrate.

* * *

Shawn opened his eyes, blinked, and took a deep breath. His body felt numb and tingly from the tips of his toes to the hairs on his head. His nose was itching and he felt like rubbing his eyes, but his arms wouldn't move. Not even his fingers or toes. The only muscles he could control were the ones manipulating his eyelids.

The room was almost dark. Only a faint, bluish glow outlined the long, cylindrical chamber through which he was moving, ever so slowly, lying flat on his back. Black tubes with glass lenses moved up and down his body, humming from time to time, sometimes stopping on a particular area and pressing against the skin. It didn't hurt—it just tickled and made him want to scratch.

What have we gotten ourselves into? Shawn thought. *Where are we? How did we get here? Where's Lanor? . . . and Billy?* He strained but couldn't move his head. *I can't see . . . Is Billy in here too?*

At that instant a tall alien wearing a translating device appeared out of the darkness and moved to Shawn's side. "Your friend is ahead of you on the observation table. You are both safe and well. We only wish to collect data. Soon you will return to Lanor's chamber, well rested and remembering nothing of this time . . ."

* * *

Shawn sat up, rubbing his eyes and scratching his nose. He was on Lanor's bed, next to Billy, who was still sleeping soundly. Lanor was sitting at his desk, tuned into a chronicle about math. All three screens displayed equations with strange-looking symbols and numbers.

"Oh-h-h-h-h," Shawn sighed. "I feel a little dizzy." He looked over at Billy. "Wake up, Shelton."

"Do you feel better now?" Lanor greeted him, walking to the bed. "You have been sleeping for a long time." It had been about two hours.

"What happened?" Shawn asked, shaking his head as he moved to the edge of the bed. "Why were we sleeping? I don't remember getting tired."

"When the power surge flashed all the lights, you both fainted," Lanor answered. "I put you on the bed."

"What's he talking about?" Billy mumbled, stumbling as he took his first steps. "What power surge?"

"They are testing the engines and support-systems on the Shuttle Dome," Lanor continued. "It is late. We should return to the trees. My parents will be here soon."

Shawn looked at Billy and grinned. "Feels weird, huh? Waking up in somebody else's bed, not even remembering going to sleep."

"I don't even remember the lights flashing," Billy mumbled as they moved toward the door.

Lanor waited until they were both inside the staircase, reached into a small drawer under the desktop, and removed something shiny, which he hurriedly stuffed into a side pocket of his jumpsuit.

As they returned to the concealment of the little clearing under the trees, the ground vibrated slightly and the lights dimmed.

Shawn looked at Lanor. "Now what?"

"Do not worry. It is only another test." Lanor pointed to the bowls on the rock-table. "Perhaps you are hungry now?"

"I sure am," Billy answered quickly. "Even for squash."

But it didn't taste like squash this time.

"Hey, Anderson, try this stuff. Now it tastes like avocados in Mexican gravy and cheese sauce."

"You're out of it," Shawn giggled, as he sampled some for himself. "*Outrageous!* You're right!" he glanced back at the alien. "How did it change?"

"The taste differs according to your bodies' need for nourishment," Lanor smiled. "Eat!"

114

The boys shoveled it in like they hadn't eaten for days, cleaning the bowls with their fingers and then washing their hands in the stream.

Shawn splashed water on his face and cupped a drink in his hands. "Is *this* water from the hydro-plants?"

"All of our water is processed by the hydro-plants," Lanor answered.

"What about on your planet?" Billy interrupted, and then, catching himself in mid-thought, he remembered that there was no salt on Lios. "That's right—you don't have salt."

"On Lios," Lanor replied, "the hydro-plants strain radon gas from one of the oceans. Radium emanation occurs in this ocean because of a crack in the crust layer of the planet. Centuries ago, the elders adapted these plants to strain salt . . . here on earth."

"Sounds like your planet is a few years ahead of us," Shawn sighed, leaning against the big oak, shaking his hands to dry. And then, a light bulb lit up in his head. "The baseball, Shelton! We forgot about the baseball!"

CHAPTER ELEVEN

The Series of the Worlds

Lanor's eyes gleamed when Billy handed him the baseball. At first, he just held it, squeezing and turning it from side to side. "I thought it would be much heavier," he said. "What is it made of?"

"There's a picture of a baseball cut in half," Shawn was glad to say, "in this comic book we brought you. Hand me the book, Billy. I'll find it."

"What do you mean, you thought it would be heavier?" Billy asked, tossing the plastic bag to Shawn. "Have you seen a baseball before?"

"On earth television," Lanor answered, throwing the ball up a few feet in the air, catching it with his other hand. "It is very similar to a game on Lios, but earth people seem to have more fun."

Billy grinned. It was the first thing Lanor had said all morning that was good about earth. "Yeah, it's fun all right—especially when you're winning. Toss it over here, Lanor!"

Lanor threw the ball, underhanded, well over Billy's head. Billy stretched, barely catching it with his left hand, jumping as high as he could.

"Keep it down," Billy laughed. "Slow and easy."

"I did not know how fast it would travel," Lanor replied, catching the ball and tossing it back, this time slower and much more accurate.

"Here," Shawn called. "This is how the ball is made, Lanor. This comic book shows a lot about the game."

Lanor leaned over and peered at the cross-section drawing of a baseball, made a low humming sound, and squeezed it again. "It feels hard, for something made of yarn, rubber, and cork."

"Hey—pitch it back!" Billy yelled.

Lanor turned and tossed it over to where Billy had moved, near the edge of the clearing. Shawn dropped the comic on the table and eagerly joined in, running to the far corner, forming a wide triangle between the three.

The alien's long fingers proved very adept at throwing and catching the baseball. Soon he was tossing it overhanded, with a confident flick of the wrist, like he'd been doing it for years.

They threw the ball back and forth for a half-hour or so, until Billy finally missed a catch and went looking for it in the dense, brambly bushes. Taking advantage of this break, Shawn and Lanor both ran to the table, grabbed a tube-glass, and scurried over to the stream.

"I guess they get just as thirsty as we do," Shawn thought, swallowing the cold water. "This is great," he laughed, dunking his head in the stream. *"Yee-o-o-u-w!"* he screeched, shaking his wet hair like a dog, splashing some of the chilly water on the alien.

Lanor laughed and retaliated with a few well-aimed splashes at Shawn.

"Hey!" Billy yelled. "Wait for me!" He ran over, a little too fast, and skidded in the soft soil—right into the stream. Before long, the three of them were laughing so hard they couldn't talk, thrashing about in the icy water, doing belly-flops and back-busters.

The fun ended only with their complete exhaustion, as they crawled onto the bank, panting.

"I have had good times like this with the dolphin," Lanor grinned. "But never with a . . . friend."

"How did you meet the dolphin?" Shawn asked.

117

"I was in my ninth year when the dolphin came to me in Sector 3," Lanor answered. "He came day after day, talking the whistling language. One day, my father was with me. He spoke to the dolphin in the whistling language. I was surprised, and asked him how I could learn to speak it."

"Incredible," Billy mumbled to himself.

"Father brought me a language chronicle from the Scientific-Resource Library," Lanor continued.

Billy sat up. "Talking about science," he began, "if you don't have many trees on Lios, how do you get oxygen to breathe?"

"Synthetic oxygen, mixed with oxygen from the many hybrids we have shuttled there over the centuries."

"Synthetic?" Billy quizzed.

"Made by a chemical process."

"Oh. And where do you live?" Billy went on. "I didn't see any buildings in the chronicles of Lios."

"Father says that most of the population of Lios live in domes, like this one, under the oceans. Only the agricultural elders and city workers live on land."

"You're kidding," Billy marveled.

"The domes are much larger and interconnected with the cities by tunnels and surface craft. Mother says it is very pleasant."

Shawn gazed up through the branches, his thoughts wandering. *Well,* that *doesn't sound so hot to me,* he thought. *Give me the wide open beaches and blue sky any day.*

Billy continued. "You said the other day that you'd gone with the elders to gather specimens. How could you have done that without people seeing you?"

"We only gather specimens during the time when this side of the planet is facing away from your star," Lanor answered. "Always in darkness. But when we were seen by humans, they were taken aboard the Shuttle Dome and given medicine that altered their short-term memory, so they would have no recollection of seeing us."

One of his big eyes twitched nervously, as he turned to Shawn. "I was never allowed to see any of the humans taken aboard, and the elders did not discuss in my presence what they did with them."

"So," Shawn returned to the conversation, "you've never been on the surface of our planet during daylight hours?"

"Only the surface above our domes," he continued. "Many times, the dolphin led me there. It was very bright and warm. The air was thicker, hard to breathe. I *did* enjoy the warm feeling of your sun on my face."

"You mean you've never even been on the beach?" Billy asked, scratching his head.

"No," the alien sighed.

"Well," Billy winked at Shawn. "I have an idea."

"What now, Shelton?"

Billy grabbed a twig and began to draw in the dark soil. "This is the coastline," he began, "and this is where your domes are." He drew the outline of the canyon and domes.

Lanor bent over, studying the crude map in the dirt. "Yes," he said. "This canyon opens up again . . . farther out."

"Back here," Billy went on, "there are three sandbars." He scratched three lines, indicating their position. "You know . . . where the sand comes up real shallow, like a long hill under the surface."

"I understand," Lanor replied, perhaps a bit insulted. "I have studied the geology chronicles. Sandbars are found near many coastlines on earth, and on Lios."

"Anyway, these sandbars are so shallow in places, you can stand up . . . and it's only chest deep."

"What are you getting at, Shelton?"

"Give it a chance, Shawn," Billy grinned, and then looked directly into the alien's big eyes. "Lanor," he said, "why don't you swim in with us today?"

Lanor immediately smiled and cocked his head, first to one side, then to the other, humming low notes.

"Really!" Billy insisted. "It's your last day on earth, right? You'll be leaving tonight. Don't you want to see what it's like up there?"

Lanor stood up. "We will go," he said.

"Now you're talking," Billy jumped up.

"But," the alien continued, "we will go in the micro-sub. There is something I must show you."

"What?" Shawn asked.

"The Valley of the Eels."

"Not eels!" Shawn cringed. "No more eels . . . please!"

"We will be safe," he reassured them. "You will see one of the reasons we are leaving earth."

"All right!" Billy yelled, springing to his feet. "Here, Lanor . . . catch!" He tossed the ball.

"It's for you," Shawn said. "And the comic book is yours too!" He handed Lanor the plastic bag.

"You are *giving* me this baseball?" Lanor questioned, cocking his head.

"Sure," Billy grinned. "Get some of your friends together when you're back on Lios. Everybody likes a good game of baseball."

"I am grateful," Lanor nodded. "It is fun throwing the ball. I will cut a stick to hit it."

"That's called a bat," Shawn laughed. "You'll find out all about it when you read the book."

Lanor laughed with them as he stuffed the plastic bag with the ball and the comic into his backpack. He hadn't yet discovered the baseball cards.

"You know," Billy said as he slung his tank-harness over his shoulder and grabbed the rest of his gear. "I'll bet we live to see the day when there really *will* be inter-planetary baseball championships."

"Yeah," Shawn added. "Then it'll really be the World Series — or, better yet, the Series of the Worlds!"

CHAPTER TWELVE

The Valley of the Eels

The submarine was in another pond near the edge of the dome. It looked like a big silver manta ray, floating on the surface. A narrow walkway led to a circular hatch on top of the tail section.

Billy followed Lanor into the hatch, glancing back at Shawn and whispering, "Here we go again."

"Hey, this is going to be *great!*" Shawn beamed. "Look at this thing . . . it's outrageous!"

Inside the sub, Lanor was already in his seat, turning knobs and flipping switches. The hatch closed magically as Shawn laid his air-tank and gear next to Billy's and climbed into a chair. Oval glass viewports faced out in all directions.

"What if the elders see the sub?" Billy asked.

"They will not see us," Lanor assured them, touching several light cells on the control panel in front of his chair.

WH-I-I-E-E-E-N-N-G! WH-I-I-E-E-E-N-N-G! The sub vibrated with such intensity that it tickled Shawn's lips.

And then, the micro-sub started moving. Lanor wasn't steering anything. In fact, he wasn't even looking ahead.

"Does this thing know where it's going?" Shawn nudged Lanor.

"The coordinates for the valley have been set in the guidance system," the alien answered, fidgeting with a panel on his chair arm.

The sub slid effortlessly through a wide tunnel and out of the dome.

"Hey!" Billy piped up. "We're on the other side of the dome. How'd you do that?"

Lanor smiled but did not answer. He touched a button on his control panel, and the lights inside the sub darkened to a soft blue glow. Now the underwater realm around them seemed clearer and brighter. Shawn could even see tiny organisms he'd never noticed before.

"Is this some kind of special glass?" he asked.

Lanor flipped a switch, and the organisms vanished. "It was set for 500 power magnification," he answered.

"You can change it to a magnifying glass with the flip of a switch?" Billy leaned over. He couldn't believe his eyes.

Lanor smiled, flipped it to high magnification, then back to normal.

* * *

Back at the Dive Shop, Alfred was playing detective. He had been there since they opened, helping Bob fill air tanks and check the rental equipment. He even swept out the tank room.

"Say, Bob," he said, returning the broom to its appropriate corner. "Didn't you work out on the oil rigs a couple of summers ago?"

"Sure did, Alfred. Three months. Made enough to buy my truck. But, that's no life for me," he laughed, glancing at Alfred. "Thinkin' about bein' a rigger some day?"

"No way," Alfred shook his head.

"I can't remember ever bein' as tired an' dirty as I

122

was *that* summer," Bob sighed.

"Guess they use a lot of *detergent* out there, huh?"

"Detergent?" Bob frowned. "Same stuff I use here."

"Really?" Alfred probed. "I thought they'd probably get detergent in big fifty-gallon drums?"

"Where'd you get that idea?"

"I . . . uh . . ." he stalled, wondering if he should say anything about Gull's Island. "I was fishing out on the jetties the other day, and I saw one of the supply boats with detergent drums, so . . . I just figured . . ."

"A supply boat? With *drums* of detergent?" Bob questioned, rubbing his chin. "They don't get that stuff in drums. Comes in cardboard cases."

"Bob!" Mr. Johnson's voice buzzed from an intercom speaker on the wall. "Got a fella up here needs to rent some gear!"

Alfred hurried to get one last question in before Bob left. "Did you ever see a bald-headed supply boat captain . . . with a long black beard?"

Bob stopped short of the door and looked back. "Ya mean old 'chrome-dome'? Solid black boat from bow to stern?"

"Yeah, that's it!"

"He's bad news, Alfred. Stay clear of him."

Alfred stared at the door as it swung shut. "Bad news, huh?" he mumbled.

* * *

Shawn tightened his grip on the chair as the microsub banked sharply and soared upward, narrowly missing the back wall of the canyon.

"Yikes," he sighed under his breath, trying not to look shaken.

Billy cupped his hand over his mouth. That turn had been too much like a roller-coaster, and his stomach didn't like it one bit.

Lanor didn't notice. He just smiled. "Exhilarating!" he exclaimed.

123

Seconds later, the sub veered and leveled off briefly before dropping into another wide canyon. A murky brown liquid clouded the water.

"Something's down there!" Billy perked up. "It's a . . . ship, isn't it, Lanor? A big cargo ship."

Lanor nodded and pressed a white button. Instantly, floodlights shone in all directions.

"Crimony!" Shawn cringed. "Do you see what I see?"

Billy was looking out a different porthole, but the view was the same.

"Eels," he grimaced. "Thousands of them."

And then, in the same millisecond, they both realized *what* the eels were slithering in and out of.

"CRATES!" they shrieked.

* * *

"Mr. Johnson," Alfred broke in. He had been waiting patiently. "Can I talk to you for a minute?"

Alfred told the old man the whole story about their secret hangar, and the crates on the pier, and Blackbeard. He told them how the three of them had overheard the captain's radio conversation, and how the sailors had chased after them, like they had something to hide.

Mr. Johnson listened intently until Alfred had finished, and then turned to Bob, raising one eyebrow, winking with the other.

"I've heard some whoppers in my time," he chuckled. "But this one takes the cake."

"It's the truth!" Alfred insisted. "Shawn and Billy saw it too!"

"I don't see Shawn and Billy here backin' you up," Bob grinned.

"Alfred," Mr. Johnson said, putting his hand on the boy's shoulder. "You've told us so many stories over the years . . . you oughta write a book."

"I tell you it really happened! Something weird's going on over there!"

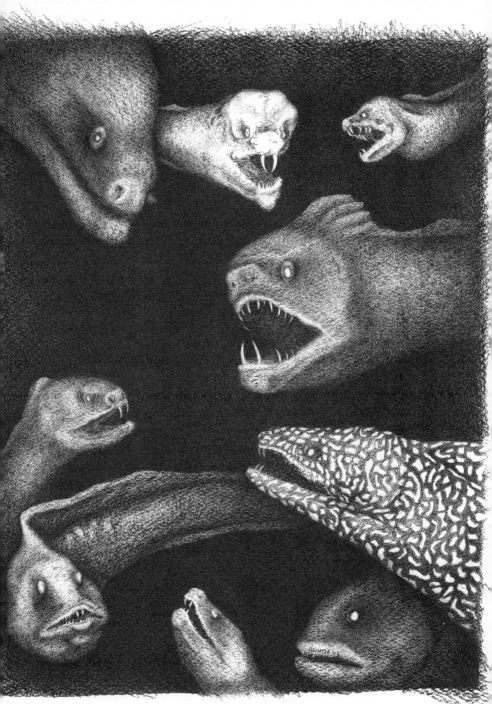

Eels were slamming into the sub, biting at the glass.

* * *

"The cargo," Lanor began, "and the crates contain radioactive waste. Nothing has survived in this valley, except the eels."

"They look so *gross*," Billy said, "and mean."

"They are mutants of many types of eels that once shared this valley with hundreds of species of plants and marine animals."

"How long has this ship been here?" Billy quizzed. "It doesn't look very old."

"The hull shattered on that ridge," he pointed to the highest elevation of the far side of the canyon, "three years ago. The dumping started soon after."

"We've seen the boat that brings these detergent drums . . . right, Shawn?"

"It is not detergent," Lanor said, flipping the switch that actuated the high-magnification glass. The tiny organisms they had seen earlier weren't there. Only little dead-looking twigs remained. He flipped it back to normal. "Your scientists are not wise to let this happen. The oceans are too precious."

"The scientists," Shawn mumbled to himself, "probably don't know about this part of their nuclear reactors."

Lanor turned and looked deep into Shawn's eyes. It was almost hypnotic. He took a piece of shiny gray paper from his side pocket and placed it in the palm of Shawn's left hand.

"This is a chart of our galaxy," he said. "Perhaps it will help you someday. Perhaps you will be an astronomer . . . or perhaps one of the first space-travelers to find Lios."

"Thanks," Shawn grinned. "I guess that could be possible . . . someday. But," he laughed, "Billy and I aren't too good at math. We'd have to work pretty hard to make those grades."

"That's the truth," Billy agreed. "Algebra's hard."

"I study because I want to be a scientist, like my

126

father, and explore the other water planets."

"What other water planets?" Shawn asked.

"The chronicles list more than one hundred other solar systems with the potential for planets like earth and Lios . . . with atmospheres and water cycles."

"For real?" Billy mumbled. "That many?"

BAP! . . . WHAP! . . . BING! . . . bing . . . bing . . . WHAP! Eels were slamming into the sub, biting at the glass.

"Whoa!" Shawn jerked back.

Lanor punched in a quick series of commands on his control panel. The sub eased up and glided away.

* * *

Alfred sped out of his driveway, pedaling furiously toward the ferry, his mom's Polaroid camera tied fast to the handlebars.

"I'll show them who's telling whoppers," he grumbled. "Write a book, huh? When they see pictures they won't laugh."

Back at the Dive Shop, Mr. Johnson was answering the phone. "Yes ma'am," he said. "I'll tell him to give you a call if he shows up here . . . You're welcome." He pressed the intercom switch. "Bob, you haven't seen the Anderson boy this morning, have you?"

"No . . . just Alfred."

"Tell him to call home if you see him."

"Sure thing, Mr. J."

* * *

Leaving the polluted valley behind, Shawn turned to Billy. "I'll bet *this* is why the dolphins died."

Lanor nodded. "It is only the beginning."

Billy jumped up. "What if Cloud followed us?"

"Do not worry. The dolphin knows of the danger, and has spread the word to his kind. But . . ." he paused. "This is not the only polluted valley."

127

"What do you mean?" Shawn glanced at Billy.

"Father says there are many other places in your oceans much worse than this."

Shawn looked back at the yellowish-brown haze and mumbled to himself, "Blackbeard."

*　*　*

"What's going to happen to this dome, since you're all leaving tonight?" Billy asked as they passed the huge glass structure. "It will remain. Father says that in less than a year, barnacles and sea algae will cover the pod, and it will become part of the ocean floor."

"But, then," Shawn questioned, "why hasn't it been covered with algae and barnacles all these years?"

"An extremely high-pitched sonic vibration prevents any life growth on the glass."

"What about the trees?" Billy burst in. "They'll die."

"Yes . . . everything will return to its natural state."

"Wow," Billy sighed, "an alien shipwreck." And then, suddenly, an idea sparked through his brain. "Hey, Lanor," he said, "have you ever seen any old shipwrecks down here? Besides that cargo ship back there."

Lanor reached under the control panel, brought out a tiny glass pyramid, and slipped it into a slot on the side. A portion of the panel lit up showing a chart of the area. He studied the chart for just a second or two, and then punched in a series of coordinates.

"All right!" Billy couldn't contain himself. "Are we going to one, Lanor?"

Shawn glanced down at his watch. "One fifteen," he gasped. "That can't be right!"

"What?" Billy leaned over to see for himself. "My God, Shawn! We've been here . . . four hours! How could that be?"

Lanor jerked around and interrupted. "You speak of your God . . . Do you mean the Creator of the universe?"

Billy's eyes widened. "Yeah," he answered, caught

off-balance by Lanor's question. "Do your people believe in God? I mean . . . I guess I just never thought . . ."

Lanor straightened his neck haughtily. "Yes, we know of the Creator of the universe. Lios *is* in the only universe *we* know of . . . as is earth." He looked deep into Shawn's eyes. "I am glad to hear *you* speak of the Creator. I have seen in the chronicles of your earth that some of your scientists believe that everything in the universe just happened — without a Creator." He laughed. "How could any intelligent being believe that the intricate balance of nature just happened?" He laughed again, and the boys joined in.

After minutes of laughter, a special kind of silence came over them, and then Shawn spoke. "Well, Lanor, we're with you on that." It was his turn to look deep into the alien's eyes. "You know, I always wondered if people on other planets believed in the Creator."

* * *

Alfred left his bike in the dunes and ran toward the pier. The cables were humming. Crates were stacked on the ramp and more were on the way.

Click! He got a shot of the ski-lift chair carrying a crate to the pier.

"Gotta get a close-up of one of those drums," he mumbled, scrambling up the steps.

Click! . . . Click! He waited for the pictures to develop. "Great!" he smiled. "These'll do fine."

But then, an all too familiar sound wiped the smile from his face. "The supply boat!" He looked at the stretch of beach between him and the dunes, then back at the approaching boat.

I'll never make it, he thought, ducking behind the crates. His heart was starting to pound. Frantically, he spun around, looking for a place to hide. "Under the pier . . . that's it! I'll have to hide under the pier." He slithered under the railing and jumped down. The boat was almost there. He ducked behind one of the pilings and waited.

"Please, God," he trembled, "don't let them see me." He stood as still as he could, holding the camera close to his chest, trying to calm the pounding.

The boat pulled up to the pier and two men jumped off, just as before, hurriedly sliding the crates across the ramp.

"Get a move on!" he heard Blackbeard growl at the men. "Daylight's burnin'..."

Minutes later, the boat engines revved. "That's enough!" the captain yelled. "We'll be makin' two trips today!"

The men jumped back on the boat as it eased away from the pier.

"Seize the day," Alfred thought to himself. He had heard it in a movie once, and thought it sounded neat.

When the engines revved again, and he could see the "rooster-tail" kicking up behind the boat, he jumped out, focused the camera, and — *Click!* ... *Click!* ... *Click!* That was it. The camera was out of film. He ducked behind the pier and waited to see if the pictures were going to come out all right.

"Yes!" he said, proud of himself. "This'll work!" The boat's name and registration number were clearly visible: "SEA TRAMP Tx 794." Also visible were the crates, stacked on the fantail.

* * *

Shawn studied the illuminated chart on the control panel while Billy gazed out the viewports.

"Which one of these symbols is your bio-pod?" Shawn asked.

Lanor pointed. "Here ... and *these* indicate the location of the remains of wrecked vessels."

"Hey!" Billy broke in. "I see something!"

The micro-sub slowed and sank gracefully to the bottom. Ahead of them lay the broken mast of an old square-rigger amid countless other shattered beams and sheets of lead. Every inch of the exposed wood was riddled with worm holes.

Shawn looked back at the chart. "Which one of these are we at now, Lanor?" he asked.

The alien traced a line with his long finger west-southwest from the bio-pod, and stopped on a series of symbols near the shoreline.

"We're *that* close to the beach?" Shawn gasped. "Shelton . . . look!"

"What?" Billy mumbled.

Shawn pointed to the bio-pod on the chart, and then slid his finger due west across the chart to the shore. "Look . . . we're not far from *our* ship rail."

Billy grinned, wider and wider, as what Shawn had said gradually sunk in. "Hey, you're right! That means . . ." he looked up at Shawn. "*Our* ship rail might be part of *this* shipwreck!"

Lanor looked at the chart and nodded. "You are correct." He cocked his head back and forth several times before continuing. "Is *this* the beach where you live?"

"We're not far from it," Shawn nodded. "Are you ready?"

Lanor didn't answer. He punched in a new set of coordinates and removed the little glass pyramid. The chart disappeared.

"This is for you, Billy," he said, handing him the tiny chronicle.

"But . . ." Billy stammered. "How can I use it? I don't have a projector."

"Perhaps someday . . . you will build one," he said, peering deep into Billy's eyes.

Billy didn't have an answer for that. But Lanor's gaze had instilled a new sense of self-confidence in him. Somehow, it didn't seem so impossible. He turned and stared out at the shipwreck as the sub rose slowly and turned west-northwest.

"Yeah . . ." he murmured, "maybe I will."

131

* * *

Alfred sat on his bike at the ferry landing, nervously waiting . . . and waiting . . . and waiting.

"What's the deal?" he grumbled, looking across the channel at the motionless ferries on the other side. "Come on, let's get the show on the road!" He shielded his eyes from the glaring sun and squinted to see what the hold-up was.

"Oh, great!" he mumbled. A big gas truck was slowly inching its way onto one ferry. The other ferry was shutting down for the afternoon slack-time. He would just have to wait.

"Cat livers! This *would* have to happen now!"

* * *

The sub slid up onto the outer slope of the third sandbar and stopped, just below the surface. Lanor flipped a switch and the hatch on the tail section periscoped up through the surface and opened.

"We'd better put our gear on," Shawn said, jumping over the chair. Billy followed.

Shawn turned inward as he donned his gear. *Is all this* really *happening?* he thought. *Am I* really *in an alien's submarine?* He pinched his arm.

Billy was the first one out. *"Unreal!"* he yelled back through the hatch. "Cloud is here!"

"You're kidding," Shawn smiled, crawling up the ladder. "Lanor!" he called back, as soon as he saw him. "It's the dolphin!"

"Why do you call the dolphin 'Cloud'?" he asked as he joined the boys, standing waist deep on the submerged sub. The surf had gone flat.

"The marking on his back," Billy replied. "But then, I guess you don't see many clouds down there, do you?"

Shawn wasn't listening. He was checking out the beach in all directions, hoping it would be deserted. If anyone saw them crawling out of a hatch on the sandbar,

132

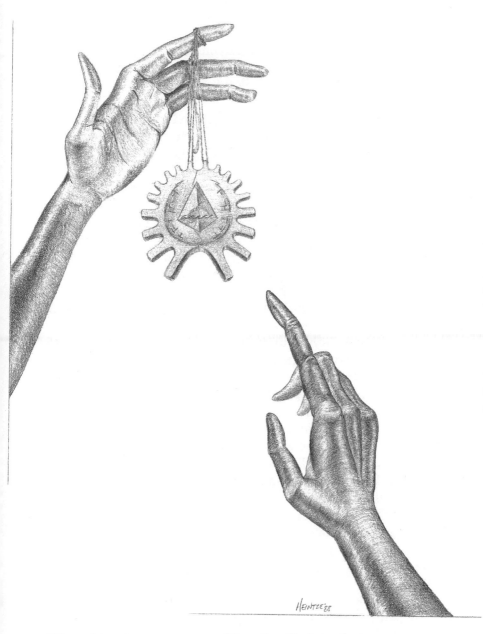

"Wear this when you come to Lios. It will show that you are a friend of our planet."

133

and with Lanor . . .

"You know what *I* think?" he said. "*I* think we'd better get in the water before anyone spots us."

"I think you're right," Billy agreed, sliding off the sub
toward the dolphin. "Hi, Cloud! How'd you know we'd be
here?"

Just then, a speck of light flashed from somewhere in
the dunes. Lanor jerked his head and panned the beach.
"Is *that* the pod you live in?" he asked, focusing in on a
beach house nestled in the dunes.

"No, I live over there. You can barely see the roof . . .
the brown one . . . with the two chimneys."

"Come on, Lanor," Billy called. "Get down in the water!"

The alien cocked his head back and forth, glanced
between the boys and the beach, and reached into his
side pocket. He motioned for the boys to come closer, as
he slid into the water.

"*This* is for you," he said, opening his hand to reveal
a shiny gold medallion on a double chain. It sparkled in
the sun as he held it up with one hand, pointing to it with
the other. "Wear this when you come to Lios. It will show
that you are a friend of our planet." He gestured for them
to look closer, and pressed his thumbs on two raised por-
tions of the medallion. There was a soft *click* as he pulled
it apart. It separated into two equal parts, jagged in the
middle. He handed one of the halves to Shawn, the other
to Billy. "Friends," he said, and then looked at the dolphin. Cloud nodded his head up and down and sounded,
"Friend . . . Friend."

"Thanks, Lanor." Billy gleamed. "I've never had anything this important . . . and . . . so different."

"Really!" Shawn added, looking deep into the alien's
big peepers. "Friend . . . I hope we *do* get to come to Lios
someday."

Lanor answered with a big grin, resting his left hand
on Shawn's shoulder, his right hand on Billy's.

"I have only known you for a few days," he began.
"But you are my best friends." With this, he turned and

touched the dolphin's head. "Come . . . we must return." He climbed back onto the sub and into the hatch, stopping halfway in to wave one last time. "Study the math and science!" he said. "Find Lios, my friends! I will be waiting for you!"

Before they could reply, he disappeared and the hatch closed. Seconds later, it sank out of sight, and was gone.

Shawn felt a fluttering sensation in his chest that he had only felt once before, when his grandmother died. His eyes welled up, and tears trickled down his cheeks.

They stood there, staring out into the Gulf, a good ten minutes or so before Billy finally broke the silence.

"Weird, huh?" he sighed.

Shawn smiled. "Yeah. But it's a good weird. Let's go."

"See ya someday, Lanor," Billy mumbled, as they turned and waded in, holding up their shiny gifts from another planet, sparkling in the afternoon sun.

"You know," Shawn sighed, as they stepped onto the beach and started unstrapping their tanks. "We really *have* to do something about Blackbeard."

"You mean spill the beans about Lanor and the Valley of the Eels?"

"No, of course not. We don't have to let on that we know *where* he's dumping the stuff. All we have to say is that we saw him loading crates over on Gull's Island. And we think it's drugs."

"Drugs?"

"Yeah, then they'll go after him for sure."

"And when they do," Billy perked up, "they'll find out that he's *really* hauling radioactive waste! Yeah . . . that sounds good!"

"Alfred's going to be bummed that we ruined his secret place, though," Shawn mumbled. "But what else can we do? We *can't* let old Blackbeard keep dumping that junk out there!"

"He'll understand when he finds out what's going on."

"I hope so. I was just starting to like the guy."

135

"Yeah," Billy agreed. "He's not such a jerk after all. But who are we going to tell . . . the police?"

Shawn thought for a while. "No, let's see what Mr. Johnson thinks first. Come on," he said, grabbing his gear, "let's hitch a ride to the Dive Shop!"

CHAPTER THIRTEEN

A Glint of Light

Mr. Johnson flinched as he listened to Shawn describe what they had seen on Gull's Island. He and Bob exchanged glances but remained silent until Shawn said that he suspected the crates were full of drugs.

"Well, son," he said. "Them's pretty strong words."

"Sounds like the same story Alfred told us, though," Bob interrupted.

"Alfred?" Billy exclaimed.

"He already *told* you?" Shawn quizzed, feeling a bit relieved.

"It wouldn't surprise me if old 'chrome-dome' was up to no good," Bob went on. "They busted him for smugglin' illegal aliens just last year."

"I remember," Mr. Johnson mumbled, twisting his mustache nervously.

At that instant, Alfred burst through the back door of the shop, yelling, "Bob . . . Mr. J! I've got pictures!"

* * *

The rest of the afternoon was exciting, to say the least. Alfred's pictures did the trick. Mr. Johnson called the Coast Guard and, within the hour, Blackbeard was caught red-handed three miles off the coast, dumping crates.

At the boys' request, Mr. Johnson said that he had received an anonymous tip, so no one would get into any trouble for trespassing on government property.

Hours later, as Shawn and Billy sat glued to the television set for the 6:00 P.M. news, Mr. Anderson walked in.

"What's up?" he asked, plopping down in his favorite chair. "Anything interesting happen today?"

"They figured out what killed the dolphins," Shawn answered, sneaking a wink at Billy.

"Is that right? What was it?"

"They caught some schmuck dumping radioactive waste three miles out," Billy replied.

"Radioactive waste?"

"Yeah," Shawn went on. "They say it's probably the reason behind all the fish kills we've been having lately."

"My God," Mr. Anderson mumbled, shaking his head. "What next?" He leaned back, unfolding the evening paper. "Did you see your dolphin today, son?"

"We sure did, Dad. He's fine."

"I just hope they can get all that mess cleaned up before any *more* dolphins wander into it," Billy sighed.

"Look, Dad! Mr. J.'s on TV!"

The news reporter was interviewing Mr. Johnson in front of the Dive Shop.

"Pretty neat, huh, Dad! Mr. J. turned them in!"

"What?" Mr. Anderson sat up, raising the volume with his remote control.

"I found these pictures in the mailbox this mornin'," the old man was saying. "Then I got an anonymous call this afternoon explainin' what they was all about. The Coast Guard did all the work . . . I just passed on the information."

"Such a deal," Mr. Anderson smiled. "Old Mr. Johnson, on the six o'clock news."

The boys exchanged glances, biting their lips to keep from grinning.

"Come on, Shelton," Shawn stood up. "Let's go out back and throw the frisbee."

. . . suddenly, it shot straight up into the
deep darkness of space.

139

"Are you going to show the medallion to your dad?" Billy asked as the screen door slammed shut behind them.

"You recognized it too . . . Didn't you?"

"If you mean that it's just like the one we found with your dad's old gear," he said, almost whispering, "yeah . . . I recognized it. They *must* have found the domes that day with Mr. Johnson."

"Right," Shawn whispered, even though no one was around to hear. "They probably swore themselves to secrecy like we did. Or maybe the aliens gave them some of that medicine Lanor was talking about—the stuff that makes humans forget."

"Well," Billy said. "*Are* you going to show it to your dad?"

"No . . ." Shawn paused. "Like I said before, he has his secrets . . . and we have ours."

* * *

It was 2:00 A.M. and Shawn hadn't slept a wink. He was out on the porch roof again, peering into the clear, starlit sky, when a glint of light near the horizon caught his eye. At first the light had a bluish glow, but as it moved diagonally across the sky, it changed from blue to red to yellow—and then, back to blue.

That has to be the Shuttle Dome, he thought, squinting his eyes, trying to keep the light in focus. It continued to change from blue to red to yellow, as it traveled across the sky until, suddenly, it shot straight up into the deep darkness of space.

Huge, fluttering butterflies invaded his stomach as he sat, staring into the patch of black infinity where the light had disappeared. He thought about Lanor and his glass chronicles.

Amazing, he thought. *It's like Lanor said — even*

140

though we've only known each other a few days, it feels like we've always known him. I guess time isn't what makes a good friendship. He pulled the star chart from his pocket and spread it out on the roof. *I keep getting this overwhelming feeling that I* will *travel to Lios—someday.* He vowed to himself, right then and there, not to think of his studies as difficult or boring, but rather as a key to get to Lios. "I'll sure try, Lanor," he mumbled.

Holding the medallion in the light that spilled from his bedroom window, he wondered aloud: "What *is* it about this thing—and the star chart?" He laid it on the chart, turning it first one way, then another. "When Lanor held the medallion up and said 'Lios,' he had a peculiar look in his eyes that—"

Then he saw it. "But what's this supposed to mean?" he gasped.

THE END?

or

IS IT ONLY THE BEGINNING?

Glossary

actuate (v) 1. to put into action 2. to move to action

ammonia (n) 1. a colorless, gaseous compound of nitrogen and hydrogen 2. a solution (ammonia water) of ammonia in water

amplify (v) 1. to increase (voltage, current, or power) in magnitude or strength 2. to make louder

anonymous (adj) 1. of unknown or undeclared origin or authorship

astronomer (n) 1. a scientist who studies the celestial bodies and their magnitudes, motions, and constitutions (celestial bodies = planets, stars, etc.)

barnacle (n) 1. a marine crustacean that is free-swimming when young but fixed (as to rocks) when adult

barrage (n) 1. a heavy, prolonged attack of words, blows, sounds

belaying pin (n) 1. a removable wooden or metal pin in the rail of a ship, around which ropes can be fastened

binoculars (n) 1. a hand-held telescope which has lenses for both eyes

buoy (n) 1. a floating object anchored in water to mark something (as a channel)

caulk (v) 1. to make tight against leakage by using a sealing substance

chronicle (n) 1. a historical record of facts or events arranged in the order in which they happened 2. a narrative history

conch (n) 1. the large spiral, one-piece shell of any of various sea mollusks

concoction (n) 1. combination of various ingredients; compound

copasetic, copecetic (adj) 1. good, satisfactory, excellent

corpse (n) 1. a dead body

curator (n) 1. a person in charge of a museum, library, or other collection

current (n) 1. a flow of water or air, especially when strong or swift, in a definite direction 2. a flow within a larger body of water or mass of air

cylinder (n) 1. a tubular-shaped object, the ends of which are parallel and equal circles

deplete (v) 1. to empty wholly or partly

deteriorate (v) 1. to make or become worse or lower in quality

dilapidated (adj) 1. falling to pieces or into disrepair 2. broken down, shabby, neglected

dislodge (v) 1. to force from a position or place where lodged, hiding, etc.; to drive out

*dna (v) 1. go away or leave

doubloon (n) 1. an obsolete Spanish gold coin which varied in value from about $5 to about $16

emanate (v) 1. to come forth or give off heat, light, radiation, etc.

embankment (n) 1. a raised structure to hold back water or carry a roadway

exhilarate (v) 1. to make cheerful, merry, or lively 2. to invigorate or stimulate

fantail (n) 1. the part of the main deck at the stern (back) of a ship

fathom (n) 1. a length of six feet, used as a unit of measure for the depth of water or the length of a rope or cable

fuse (v) 1. to unite as if by melting together; to blend

galleon (n) 1. a large Spanish ship of the fifteenth and sixteenth centuries, with three or four decks at the stern; used as both a warship and a trader

gargantuan (adj) 1. gigantic; huge

genetics (n) 1. the branch of biology that deals with heredity (what is passed down through generations) of related animals and plants

geology (n) 1. the science dealing with the physical nature and history of the earth, including the structure and development of its crust, the composition of its interior, individual rock types, the forms of life found as fossils, etc.

gradual (adj) 1. proceeding or changing by steps or degrees 2. developing little by little

144

grouper (n) 1. any of several large fishes found in warm seas

helm (n) 1. the wheel or tiller by which a ship is steered

hodgepodge (n) 1. any jumbled mixture; mess; medley

horizon (n) 1. the line where the sky seems to meet the earth

hybrid (n) 1. the offspring produced by crossing two individuals of unlike genetic constitution 2. the offspring of two plants or animals of different races, varieties, species, etc.

hydro-plants (n) 1. plants containing water

hydroelectric (adj) 1. producing, or having to do with the production of, electricity by water power or by the friction of water or steam

hypnotically (adj) 1. causing a sleeplike condition physically induced, usually by another person, in which the subject is in a state of altered consciousness and responds to the suggestions of the hypnotist

illuminate (v) 1. to brighten; to light up

impending (adv) 1. about to happen; imminent

incessant (adj) 1. never ending; continuing or being repeated without stopping in a way that seems endless; constant

intercoastal canal (n) 1. between two coastlines, as with the waterway between the mainland and barrier island

irrational (adj) 1. lacking the power to reason 2. senseless; unreasonable; absurd

*jkewdaab (v) 1. hurry

luminescent (n) 1. giving off any cold light; specifically, fluorescence or phosphorescence

meander (n) 1. pattern of winding or crisscrossing lines 2. aimless wandering; rambling

millisecond (n) 1. a unit of time equal to one-thousandth of a second

nuclear reactor (n) 1. a device for initiating and maintaining a controlled nuclear chain reaction in a fissionable fuel for the production of energy

pedestal (n) 1. the foot or bottom support of a column, pillar, vase, lamp, statue, etc.

perimeter (n) 1. the outer boundary of a figure or area; as in, *a fence marked the perimeter of the field* 2. circumference

pivot (n) 1. a point, shaft, pin, etc. on which something turns 2. to make a pivoting movement (v)

plight (n) 1. a dangerous or awkward situation; predicament

145

pristine (adj) 1. still pure or untouched; uncorrupted; unspoiled

pulsate (v) 1. to beat or throb rhythmically, as the heart 2. to vibrate; quiver

radioactive waste (n) 1. liquid, solid, or gaseous waste resulting from mining of radioactive ore, production of reactor fuel materials, reactor operation; from use of radioactive materials in research, industry, and medicine

reef (n) 1. a line or ridge of rock or sand lying at or near the surface of the water; shoal

reforestation (n) 1. the process of planting new trees on land once forested

regulator (n) 1. a device, as with scuba gear, used to control the flow of air from the tank to the mouthpiece

retaliate (v) 1. to return like for like; to return evil for evil; to pay back after being wronged or hurt

retract (v) 1. to draw back or in 2. withdraw or disavow; recant or revoke

sandbar (n) 1. a ridge or narrow shoal of sand formed in a river or along a shore by the action of currents or tides

sarcastically (adv) 1. making a remark in a taunting, sneering, cutting, or caustic way

scuba (n) 1. equipment worn by divers for breathing underwater, consisting typically of one or two compressed air tanks strapped to the back and connected by a hose to a mouthpiece (stands for Self Contained Underwater Breathing Apparatus)

sonar (n) 1. an apparatus that transmits high-frequency sound waves through water and registers the vibrations reflected from an object, used in finding submarines, depths, etc. (similar to dolphin's echolocation)

starboard (n) 1. the right-hand side of a ship or airplane as one faces forward, toward the bow; opposed to port

succumb (v) 1. to give way to; yield; submit 2. to die

telepathy (n) 1. supposed communication between minds by some means other than the normal sensory channels; transference of thought

transparent (adj) 1. clear; capable of being seen through

treading water (v) 1. swimming to keep the body upright and the head above water as by moving the legs in a treading motion without moving forward

146

trespass (v) 1. to go onto another's land or property without permission or right 2. to intrude or encroach

turbulent (adj) 1. full of commotion or wild disorder; turmoil 2. unruly or boisterous

uncanny (adj) 1. being mysterious or unfamiliar, especially in such a way as to frighten or make uneasy; eerie; weird

undulate (v) 1. to cause or to move in waves; swinging

veer (v) 1. to change directions; shift; turn or swing around

vintage (adj) 1. the type or model of a particular year or period; as in, *a car or plane of prewar vintage*

water plant (n) 1. any plant living submerged in water or with only the roots in or under water

* Language of Lios

147